GALWAY BAY
FOLK
TALES

T0353180

GALWAY BAY
FOLK
TALES

RAB FULTON

ILLUSTRATED BY
MARINA WILD

The
History
Press
Ireland

For Jennie, Dylan and Callum

First published 2013
Reprinted 2017

The History Press Ireland
50 City Quay
Dublin 2
Ireland
www.thehistorypress.ie

© Rab Fulton, 2013
Illustrations © Marina Wild

The right of Rab Fulton to be identified as the Author
of this work has been asserted in accordance with the
Copyrights, Designs and Patents Act 1988.

British Library Cataloguing in Publication Data.
A catalogue record for this book is available from the British Library.

ISBN 978 1 84588 779 7

Typesetting and origination by The History Press
Printed by TJ Books Limited, Padstow, Cornwall

CONTENTS

PART ONE:
ANCIENT TALES

Introduction to Part One

Hunting Yetis

I have not yet seen a yeti in Ireland, though I have been on many a yeti hunt with my two sons. A yeti is rumoured to live at the top of the hill near our home. The journey to the hill involves beating a path through long needle-sharp grass, thistles and nettles, which come up to the shoulders of my oldest son, and reach high above the head of my youngest.

As we get nearer to the hill on one such hunt the walking gets easier as the tall grasses give way to rocks, bits of bog and purple heather. The rocks have patches of lichen and moss, and the bog hosts the very occasional minute purple flower. The going is easier if a bit messier now and my oldest son explains all about yetis to my youngest: specifically that yetis are very shy and we may not get to see one. There are clues though, if you look: in particular the occasional empty can of super strong cider. Making upward progress is a slow and convoluted task as my youngest son is still not quite at the age where he can focus on one task. Distracted by a rock, flower, ant or whale-shaped cloud he wanders off and has to be retrieved.

As we go further up spikes of gorse stick out from between the heather, ready to snag and prick unsuspecting explorers, particularly pre-school age explorers. Even on the sunniest of days the wind can suddenly take a snatch at our hats.

Finally, we reach the narrow path that leads up to a huge spiky clump of gorse, which is sat like a hat or a wave or a really bad haircut right there on the very crest of the hill. This is the yeti's hideout. Inside the great bush the hill's crown has three deep dents where we can sit, sheltered from the wind and weather by the tight weave of gorse spikes and yellow, scented flowers. It is a wonderful spot for a yeti to live; a perfect three-room apartment without the bother of any mortgage repayments, a seemingly endless supply of alcohol and, overhead, the ever changing sky.

The yeti, however, is never at home, which invariably begins a discussion about where the yeti is, who he is hanging out with and what he's up to. There is a suspicion, commonly articulated by my eldest son, that the yeti keeps the company of robbers and bandits, and that he may even allow them to use his home to hide in. Such discussions are usually cut short by my youngest son climbing or rolling down into the deepest of the three hollows. His rescue is simple and swift, and never ever appreciated.

Then we push and crawl our way back outside, stand on the flat rocks on the south of the hill and take a look at the view. To the west of us can be glimpsed Connemara; to east of us, and much nearer, are the lower waters of Lough Corrib; to the south lies the great expanse of Galway Bay with the hills of the Burren opposite. Following those hills westwards and we can see lying low on the horizon the Aran Islands. Looking over from the islands our view returns us to Connemara.

Folded into this topography, like children resting in a blanket, are stories – many, many stories – waiting to be roused and sent out to play. In a little while I will tell you some of those stories, but not just yet. Stories can never start exactly on time. A little bit of anticipation is great for helping a story lift off and fly on its way. So stay with me for a moment.

SHARING STORIES

As a storyteller I hear many accounts of the strange and the wonderful. Not so long ago an acquaintance of mine encountered a *capal uisge* up in Connemara. I have stood in the summer sunshine discussing the legendary island of

Hy Brazil with people who have encountered that peculiar aberration of physics and geology. (My oldest son does not find Hy Brazil problematic in any way – how else would foxes get to other countries?) Ghosts, of course, are a common currency, and there are still young Irish who can tell you about losing a block of time after wandering into a field belonging to the good folk.

Every so often I encounter someone who tells me that storytelling is dead and Ireland empty of folk tales, or that the tales are not quite what they use to be. I can only shrug. If it weren't for the stories, and the desire to hear and share them, I would have great difficulty feeding my children. Ireland and the Irish remain brimming with stories. I have told stories in pubs, libraries, museums, schools, priests' houses, at Presbyterian gatherings, festivals, in anarchist forums, on beaches, in fields, woods, on a booming bouncing ferry boat on the way to Inis Mór …

My weekly telling takes place in a darkened room in the Crane Bar in Galway city. It is not uncommon for members of my audience to tweet or blog during my show, sharing their experience as it happens. The little rectangular pool of light from an iPod adds a lovely hint of eerie future shock to any storytelling. Cameras are also ubiquitous. All of which is perfectly fine by me. When I tell stories with storms in them I encourage the audience to take pictures to simulate lightning flashes.

But what manner of stories and where do they come from? Well, the tales I tell my children are usually the more innocent and magical ones. My eldest son's favourite is the kiddy's version I tell of 'The Axe, the Hook and The Long Sharp Knife'. My youngest son though finds this story 'Boring!'. The version in this book is for an older audience and is closer to the version I tell in my Celtic Tales show. Closer, but not quite the same …

Whilst all the stories in this book form part of my Celtic Tales show, it would be an impossible task to translate my live performances of these stories into a written form. How I tell a story on any given evening depends on many factors: the weather, my mood, the make-up of the audience: is it big or small, Irish, international or a mixture? Even when I begin telling a story there is often an element of free flowing, of veering off in strange directions, of responding to unexpected (but always welcome) audience participation. How then to write a story that encapsulates all that energy, fun and sleight of hand?

The answer of course is simple – it cannot be done. The written word and the spoken word are two very different ways of transmitting information to an audience. All I can do is make sure that, regardless of the form, I make the stories grab the audience and take them on strange and wonderful journeys.

The stories in this book cover the history of Galway Bay – add or take an eon or two – from the formation of the bay right up to modern period. There are humorous tales and angry tales; tales of magic and tales of the macabre; there are fantastic creatures and lusty adventurers; some of the tales, like the house martins who live in the eaves of my house, take journeys far over land and sea, before returning to their Galway home.

They are my take on existing tales, many of which have been around for a long time and in differing guises. Mine are no more the definitive version of these stories than anybody else's. Trying to nail down the absolute and final correct version of any story in Ireland has always been a thankless task. Even the most dedicated of folklorists can only record the version of a story that they happened to hear from the person sat in front of them. If they walked a mile up the road they would encounter a completely different version of the same tale.

In the decades before the First World War, the wonderful folklorist Thomas Johnson Westropp found issues of authenticity and originality problematic, being very alive to the fact that some tales he heard in Clare, Galway and Mayo were the result of book lore, rather than oral lore, and in his writing he often takes to tasks early folklorists for their lack of critical appraisal. And yet has there ever been a time in Irish history when the written word did not impact on the spoken, and vice versa? This is the island, after all, that prides itself on preserving Latin learning for Western Europe during the post Roman period. Only the elite may have been able to read and write but they did not live cocooned from the rest of Ireland's population. Rather, the reverse is true: those with the power and authority of the written word had a very direct impact on how Irish culture and stories developed and changed over the centuries.

Ireland, no less than any other country, has always been open to outside influences. It is up to the individual as to whether this be seen as cross fertilization or pollution, but before worrying about the purity or otherwise of stories it is well to remember that it is now a strongly held belief that Balor was a Norse creation, and I've heard it said that the pooka and the children of Lir are imports from the Auld enemy … Should we dismiss the pooka as nothing more than a shaggy goat story, and haven't Fionnuala, Aodh, Fiachra and Conn suffered enough without being given a deportation order?

Westropp also mentions the caution and reluctance he encountered from some of the communities he was hoping to get stories from. There may be a perfectly innocent reason for why some people where reluctant to talk to strangers asking questions. However, when I read Westropp I am always surprised at just how welcoming people were, given that the late nineteenth century witnessed the Land War in Ireland. The violence and convulsions of the time may explain some of the resistance he encountered – or perhaps not.

Of course the converse could equally be true, and I have long had an idea of writing a story set in Connemara where a family intent on smuggling an IRB member out the back door order the granny to tell a scéal to the fellow whose turned up at the front door with a pencil in his hand and a mouthful of questions …

But these are worries for folklorists, academics and storytellers. The reader or listener of a tale would be best to relax and enjoy the tales as they unfold. As for alcohol-dependent yetis, there are those that say there are no such things, and certainly no such things in the west of Ireland. But after you have read the stories in this collection I think you will agree that absolutely anything is possible in the little corner of our planet that is Galway Bay.

But before we get to the first tale it would do well to attempt to come to some form of an understanding about the importance of stories and storytelling. To do this we need to travel back in time a bit. Say, fourteen billion years ago or so.

ONCE UPON A TIME

Fourteen billion years ago or so there were no stars, no colours, no darkness. Nothing existed and yet the potential for everything and every combination of every possibility of everything ever did exist, all waiting to play out in countless multiverses.

Then, with a slow release of divine breath, particles – so minuscule they lacked weight or even mass – slowly spread through the realm of infinite yet-to-be possibilities. As they moved they attracted mass and form, slowed down and coalesced into the actuality of times and spaces, events and places

At some point our little speck of a solar system formed. Rocks came together, forming planets and satellites; some blessed with heat, water and organic materials such as propane, ethane and acetylene. Whilst life began on a number of planets, many of the spinning moons of the outer gas giants carried on producing the compounds from which future lives could be produced.

On the planet presently know as Earth a life form came into being that was to be the most successful, adaptable and long lasting of all the planet's inhabitants. We know such creatures by their generic name – bacteria. Despite their success, bacteria have not – as far as we know – ever produced any stories of note. For stories we have to go to a species that has only been around a little while, and if its current behaviour is anything to go by, seems to be in danger of being classified as one of the least adaptable and unsuccessful creations in all the multiverse – the naked, walking and talk talk talking ape known as *Homo sapien.*

Speech is a very peculiar pastime, all the more so when we consider that so much of our communication with others revolves around gossip and little exchanges of information that seem to be of very little consequence. However, little things can have very big ramifications, as anyone involved with the CERN project will happily tell you. CERN, as its website succinctly puts it, is the place where the 'world's largest and most complex scientific instruments are used to study the basic constituents of matter – the fundamental particles'.

You don't get much smaller – or bigger – than that. However, what the CERN website does not state is that, just like you and I and the old man next door, the researchers at CERN spend much of their talking time exchanging those little bits of trivia we refer to as gossip.

This is to be expected as gossip is the particle exchange that is fundamental to all our human ingenuity. When two or more people gossip they create a space dedicated to the intricate interweave of active silence and active sound: listening and talking. The words and silences may seem trivial, but the sound silence transference system (SSTS) serves an infinity of possible functions. SSTS serves as a form of social grooming; it also takes the focus off the more analytical part of brain, allowing it to relax and muse over whatever problems are besetting us. Crucially, SSTS serves to confirm that we are real, valid and functioning entities: we create words, someone listens to them; then they create words for us to listen to. In summary SSTS (aka gossip) is what proves we are human, lets our brains relax so they can solve BIG problems, and can strengthen existing – or create new – relationships.

There is another strange, and let's face it, creepy aspect of exchanging words, whether gossip or thesis, which is this: when we speak or when we listen we change – in an instant we can become anything; the empathetic friend, the witty seducer, the patient parent, the righteous preacher; we become the demon, the angel, the spark of all new ideas and the crusher of all dreams. We, the walking, talk talk talking ape, are the true shape-shifters. The Tuatha de Danann have nothing on us; werewolves and vampires are just irate puppies and sexually frustrated bats. With words we can soothe the deepest pain or fracture and break the will of another human being. Words are magic. They can save life and they can take life.

Whilst a full understanding of words has remained as elusive as a Higgs Boson particle, I would suggest that the power of words comes from the fact that every individual word is saturated with the innate and limitless power that existed fourteen billion years ago when there were no stars, no colours, no darkness; when nothing existed except the potential for everything and every combination of every possibility of everything …

Even used casually, words have power. When they are used with deliberation and precision that power becomes magnified a thousand fold. This is why poets and satirists in many countries live in fear of their lives; why the more intolerant practitioners of religion detest theatre. In the mouths of seasoned and bloodied practitioners words can peel back the veneer of this reality and allow the audience to glimpse an infinity of other realities and possibilities. Sometimes those who have mastered the power of words, whether it is a Martin Luther King or Adolf Hitler, can shape the destinies of entire nations and eras.

It is perhaps for the best that few of us will ever command such mastery of language. Nonetheless our words are important. With them we can construct shelters, wherein we can hide for a moment from the great narratives of history whilst sharing myths, stories, tall tales and gossip. I use all of these elements when telling my Galway stories, as well as archaeology, philosophy, history and a pinch (or two) or poetic license. All of which I have attempted to translate into the following written narrative, a narrative which begins, as all tales about Galway must, with an account of those much-maligned creatures – the giants of Connemara.

1

An Fear Mór

A long, long, *fadó*, *fadó* ago there lived on the shores of Galway Bay a giant, known as An Fear Mór, the Big Man. This fellow would wade out into the Atlantic to try and catch whales, much in the manner of children today trying to scoop up handfuls of sprats in the summer sunshine; one moment frustrated, the next delighted when finally they catch a slippery streak of silver.

Of course, where a child is happy enough to simply stare at the little baby fish flapping and twisting in the palm of his hand, a whale-snatching giant has other intentions. Each leviathan caught by An Fear Mór would be shoved wiggling and puffing into a satchel so big you could lose a village in it. Once enough beasts where caught, the giant would wade back to his home on the southern coast of Connemara known to this day as Cuan An Fhir Mhóir, the Bay of the Big Man. There he would boil up the whales in a cavity between three massive rocks known as Brannradh An Fhir Mór, the Big Man's Cauldron.

The cooking of the whales required a prodigious quantity of water, which was of course easily to hand, and an also equally prodigious quantity of timber to keep the fire going. At that time, so the archaeological record shows us, there was indeed plenty of woodland up in Connemara. Nowadays, save for the occasional cluster of trees, all that remains of the long-gone forests are the black stumps found deep in the bellies of the peat bogs.

The vanishing of the trees of Connemara has aroused much discussion and passion, with opinions divided on whether to blame human encroachment, climatic change or the culinary exploits of An Fear Mór. The Big Man may indeed have had some responsibility for the changing botany of the landscape around him. The problem, however, is that it is very difficult to examine the exploits of giants in a neutral fashion. They left no written or pictographical record, and much that we know of them comes from their human neighbours who were – and remain to this day – violently antagonistic towards any creature over sixty feet tall. The reputation of giants has been further sullied by the fact that it was not only whales that An Fear Mór plucked from the chilly Atlantic.

Much like the whales who fed and clothed the ancient Inuit, we can imagine that the migration of whales past the western seaboard of Ireland provided a source of food and materials for early human communities.[1] Pushing their fragile skin boats out from shore, the hunters would row after the great cetacean flocks. At the climax of the chase harpoons would be embedded into a whale's body. Attached to the harpoon were air-filled bladders that would slow down a wounded creature and stop it diving to safety. Tired and terrified, the creature would then be dragged and steered towards the shore and its slaughter.

The whale hunt was not only a source of food for humans; it also provided a heaving gore-spattered theatre for individual humans to display their skills and courage. It was a

place where friendships or antagonisms were amplified to an almost supernatural degree; where future stories, myths and Gods were born in those infinite seconds of absolute soul-wrenching terror, when an enraged whale's fluke fills the whole sky and seemingly nothing in existence can stop it smashing down on a flimsy boat.

But even as the men hunted and prayed, sang and laughed, screamed and roared, drenched and blood splattered, so they too were hunted – by An Fear Mór. Humans, however, are far trickier to catch than whales. *Homo sapiens* display a cunning and a tenacity for survival out of all proportion to their physical minuteness. So small are they that it is doubtful that a giant could gain any nutritional benefit from eating even a handful. But as a snack for a giant – ah well, there is nothing as tasty as a living human; the sweetness of their meat and the prickle and crack of their bones as they're crunched up.

More important than the taste of humans though, so they say, is the narcotic buzz that comes from ingesting them. For a giant there is no ecstasy to compare to the moment when all the juice and chemical soup of the *Homo sapien* body flushes through a giant's veins and slams into its brain with sparks and flashes of cosmic blasting wonderment … For this feeling a giant will hold its breath and lurk beneath the cold waves, ignoring whole nations and commonwealths of whales, just waiting and watching for the little shadows of human boats to float overhead. Then up he will come, with a leap and a gasp to grasp at the nearest of the pathetic vessels.

Humans, needless to say, have a rather negative view on being used as opiates for the massive. But from a more objective perspective it can be seen that a number of benefits accrued from a giant's taste for human flesh. It put a check on human population expansion, allowing other creatures and plants to flourish within the ecology of southern Connemara. Furthermore, the humans that were caught were usually the weakest of the hunters, which meant the strong and the wise lived longer, which in turn led to a healthier genetic make up for the whole community.

For all the controversy about giants and their relationship to humans, there can be no denying that An Fear Mór made one very positive contribution to the development of culture and society in Galway Bay, which I will now relate.

1 Douglas, M.S.V., Smol, J.P., Savelle, J.M. and Blais, J.M., 'Prehistoric Inuit whalers affected Arctic freshwater ecosystems', *Proceedings of the National Academy of Sciences*, Vol. 101, No. 6 (2004)

2

GIANT LOVE

It happened that one day another giant came calling on An Fear Mór. The historical record is a little hazy on who this other giant was, but the speculation is that the visitor was An Bhean Mhór – the Big Woman – and that the visit was of a romantic nature. Certainly, love or lust would explain what happened next.

Giants are by nature solitary creatures, rarely inclined towards friendship. Yet there comes a time when reproductive needs overcome any eremitic inclination. Deep in a giant's head neurotransmitters suddenly flash like lightning in a summer storm, lust and love goes whistling through the great pipes and valves of its heart, the creature's mouth dries up, and its oxters and groin sweat out the foulest of secretions. Many miles, mountains, valleys and lakes away, another of the creatures catches the scent and, regardless of what they are doing or thinking (if indeed giants can be said to think at all), they will immediately turn windward and begin the long, slow lumbering journey towards procreation.

Rocks play a large part in the mating ritual of giants: lifting them, biting them, crushing them and of course throwing them. So it was that An Fear Mór and his lady visitor played around in the local mountains, breaking bits off here, sticking a few extra bits on there. At the climax of all this horse play, they decided to have a throwing competition. As a display of prowess each would attempt to hurl an enormous boulder over the expanse of Galway Bay and land it on to Black Head at the very tip of County Clare.

So it was that each of the two giants gouged out a hill, raced down to the water's edge and, with a roar, hurled their missiles upwards and outwards. Up and up the projectiles flew, defying gravity and smacking into the clouds. Birds screeched in terror, the very air boomed in protestation, and still the great boulders flew up. Once, twice and thrice the great stones circumnavigated the earth, skimming against the very edge of space, trailing flames and gassy tendrils.

Then, with a scream, down the great boulders came, landing in the Atlantic with such heat and force the waters opened like a monstrous flower with its white petals of roiling steam momentarily floating on the air. Next, with a boom that cracked mountains to the core, the scolding sea washed against the shores of Galway Bay, boiling the skin off all creatures feathered, finned or skin-covered.

The two giants, being constructed of much tougher material, were not in the slightest damaged by the boiling tsunami that crashed over them, and were no more put out than children who have been splashed a bit after hurling a couple of stones into a pond. Unlike children though, who always take delight in their mess and mayhem, the giants were not pleased by the havoc they had caused. Their intention had not been to split the seas, but to smack Black Head. When the floods subsided and the steaming clouds parted it was clear that neither boulder had made it over the bay. There were the tops of the boulders, peeking out of the waters looking for all the world like two lumpy pancakes on a plate.

One of the rocks had almost made it to County Clare, but the giants could not agree as to who had thrown it. An argument ensued, which escalated into a fight. 'Swim out,' An Fear Mór cried, 'and you'll see the furthest rock is mine.' At which he threw his erstwhile lover into the sea. With great paddling strokes the lady giant made her way out to the furthest rock. 'You blind fool,' she cried. 'This rock is mine, without a doubt.'

But An Fear Mór was not to be out done. 'Look closer, my love,' he called in his most beseeching bellow. As An Bhean Mhór bent to take a closer look, An Fear Mór grabbed a hill smaller but deadlier than any of the rocks in the water, and threw it with incredible accuracy at the bowed head of his former lady friend. So ended the romance of An Fear Mhór. The rock cracked against the female giant's skull, sending her flying out into the Atlantic. Curiously, that third rock almost reached Black Head, but not quite.

As to what happened to An Bhean Mhór, there is much speculation. Some say she was killed, stone dead, as it were. Others say that she was merely concussed and eventually came to, only to discover that she drifted all the way to America. As for the three great rocks, they still exist and are known to the world as Inis Mór, Inis Meáin and Inis Oirr – the Aran Islands.

Much later, events on these islands would play a pivotal role in the evolving civilization of Ireland, Europe and the world. But to understand how such a thing came about we need first take a look at the lives of the earliest human settlers in Ireland …

3

THE
TIME LORDS

In the beginning the people of Ireland were few in number and mostly scattered around the very fringe of this island, at the shores of the sea, such as Galway Bay, and the lakes and rivers. The rest of Ireland remained the domain of other beings with fangs and claws, or vast wings and tearing beaks. But in tandem with the world of blood and bone there existed the magical world, the masters of which were the Tuatha de Danann, the Immortals, who were capable of existing in many worlds at one and the same time.

Of course the very concept of 'time' is rendered problematic when discussing such magical beings. It is just about possible to create a linear narrative of the lives of the Tuatha de Danann, but, as time within their realm was (or perhaps is) as changeable as the wind and weather, it is incredibly difficult to work out just exactly when any given event happened. An uneventful day may pass in the lives of such beings, whilst centuries or even millennia roll over the lives, dreams and hopes of generations of mortals.

The Tuatha de Danann landed from a great armada of ships on the western shores. Between Lough Corrib and

Lough Mask these magical lords encountered the original inhabitants of Ireland, the fearsome Fir Bolg. The rival beings began a hurling match. However, sportsmanship quickly gave way to dirty play and dirty play to full combat. The slaughter was terrible on both sides, and King Nuada of the Tuatha de Danann had his hand severed from his wrist. After three days the Fir Bolg were routed and the survivors sought refuge on the islands of the Fomorians who, in turn, declared war on the Tuatha de Danann.

The humans subsisting along the lakes, rivers and coasts could not have been unaware of these ferocious clashes; they would have surely understood that the lightning and thunderstorms were the roar, din and sparks of cosmic warriors and weaponry. Earth tremors were caused by the failed attempt of Balor, the demonic one-eyed leader of the Fomorians, to tie a great chain to Ireland so as to drag it off into the middle of the ocean.

The presence of the Other was also experienced in less dramatic ways. For every ailment humans suffered a herb existed to provide relief. This knowledge was passed on through songs and rituals, as too were the questions asking what created the herbs, the storms and the seasons? It was only much later, after terrible pain and slaughter, that humans learned the history of the Tuatha de Danann; of their great battles with other beings; and of Miach the healer who was killed by his jealous father and on whose grave healing herbs first grew.

Humans must have appeared to these great lords as water fowl in a pond. They would have enjoyed our plumage, our courtships, our territorial disputes, perhaps have taken delight in those mannerisms that seemed to mimic their own. It was Manannan Mac Lir, the lord of the sea, who would have been most familiar with our species. It was on the edge of his territories that humans carved out an existence. As long as they paid tribute to him, with offerings in the lakes, rivers and shores, Manannan Mac Lir was content to let humans be.

What humans lacked in magic and brawn, they more than made up for with imagination and adaptability. Whilst the Tuatha de Danann wandered in their endless pleasant dreams, humans were busy manufacturing. Stones were transformed in the hands of men and women into dazzling technological implements and on the banks of the Lough Corrib flint was shaped into blades. The creation of such blades was a highly skilled craft in itself, but it is the potential use of such blades that give an insight into the sophistication of the people who crafted them.

In skilled hands a microlith could be used for cutting an umbilical cord, cleaning gangrenous flesh from a wound, bleeding a vein and other medicinal purposes. Likewise, other blades could be used to make ritual body markings or tattoos – using the dye from plants or shellfish for colouring, perhaps. A sharp blade would be crucial for cutting and shaping saplings into homes, baskets, creels, traps for birds and small animals. All of these technologies would need skilled craftspeople and ongoing communication within and beyond the immediate social group.

Digging holes in wetlands and edging them with stones, humans created *an fulacht fiadh* – self-filling water containers. These are the most common archaeological remains in Ireland, a good example being found in Athenry, County Galway. Into these structures hot stones were placed to heat the water. After that, the applications of these structures was only limited by human imagination. Scattered across Ireland in their thousands, different *an fulacht fiadh* could have been used for preparing the dead before burial, helping women in labour, or

the ritual cleaning of participants in faith ceremonies. Evidence suggests that they could equally have been used for dyeing cloth, brewing beer, bathing or as saunas. Far from being satisfied with the natural order, it would appear that 4,000 years ago our ancestors had created faith, fashion, alcoholic drinks, baths and spas.[1] Subsequent developments from watermills to iPhones can be seen as little more than one long footnote to that prehistoric burst of human ingenuity.

As time moved on and millennia separated stone tools from Bronze Age metallurgy, all things were in balance under the tutelage of the Tuatha. The rain knew when to fall and in what quantity, the sun when to shine, and the wind when to blow. Every creature knew its place and its position in the scheme of things: the boar foraging in the dank woods, the wolf waiting carefully behind a rock, the fish negotiating the currents and tides of the sea-ways, the bird weaving twigs and down into its nest.

We can only speculate on when humans became aware of the presence of the Immortals sharing this island. There are moments when humans experience life at its most extreme and terrifying: the birthing of a child, the shock of a terrible wound or the slow death of starvation. At such moments, fragile mortals find themselves balanced between infinite states of being and nonbeing, and are subject to flashes of both dazzling illumination and vast nothingness.

Gasping in pain, horror and ecstasy, such a human becomes aware of creatures watching them. Yet it is not hunger that motivates these watchers but something worse, for the creatures – whether wolves or wasps, swans or starlings – exhibit an awful and alien curiosity. As the delirium fades, with the mortal returning fully to this world or passing on into the infinite, the creatures lose interest. As they turn to leave, the beastly voyeurs warp and ripple and, just as they began to disappear, take on a shape that is almost human.

It was the very intimacy with death – the horror and the wonder of it – that made humans, in the long run, far more formidable beings than the Tuatha de Danann. Our ancestors worshipped gods to help them come to terms with birth and death, and with the sorrows and joys of the brief life between these two states. Three goddesses in particular helped us come to an understanding with this world and the worlds beyond. Their names were, and are, Fodla, Banba and Eiriu, the last of which would give her name to this island: Eire or Ireland.

Whilst the Tuatha observed humans in a frivolous manner, some humans were subjecting the Tuatha de Danann to a very forensic scrutiny. The mother cradling her child, the hunter nursing his healing wound, and the wanderer finally filling his thin belly would carry for the rest of their lives a disquieting certainty that they had encountered intelligence greater than ours. Once revealed, the Immortals could no longer remain hidden. As reports of these encounters increased, so too did accounts of the splendour of the clothes, dwellings and lifestyle of the Others.

The luxury, beauty and security of endless life of these great lords were something to emulate, but how to gain what the Tuatha de Danann had? That was the question. Amongst the first nations of this island, voices whispered that the persistent threat of hunger and fear would only end once humans were as great as the Tuatha de Danann. It is impossible at this distance in time to guess when the whispers evolved into a common currency of belief. As a belief it was harmless enough, if not indeed beneficial – what harm could there be in becoming like the Tuatha?

1 Mullal, Erin, 'Letter from Ireland: Mystery of the Fulacht Fiadh', *Archaeology Magazine*, Vol. 65, No. (2012)

4

HY BRAZIL

Of all the Tuatha de Danann, only one seems to have taken serious note of the evolution of human society. Manannan Mac Lir was always the outsider of the Tuatha de Danann and, like many an outsider before and since, he used various names. As Orbsen Mac Alloid he lived the ideal life of a great lord and explored the coastline, the topography and currents of the seas, and made journeys between the islands of the eastern Atlantic.

It was Manannan Mac Lir who attempted to divert the attentions of his human neighbours away from the splendours of the Tuatha de Danann. In the guise of Lord Orbsen he spoke to a gathering of men and women of influence. Of these, one in particular was held in such esteem that already he was referred to as a king. 'These lands are no longer big enough', explained Lord Orbsen.

'There is plenty enough,' replied the king, 'further inland, in the domain of the Tuatha de Danann.'

'That is so, but it would be no easy task to wrest their lands from them.'

'Where else could we go?' asked the king's steward.

Lord Orbsen smiled and shrugged, 'Why not colonise Hy Brazil?'

The king's daughter looked at Lord Orbsen in surprise, 'Only drowning men can get to Hy Brazil.'

'Not so, it can be reached by the living, but it is not easy.'

'Why bother though?' persisted the princess. 'It is a tricky land, solid one moment and the next having no more substance than rain clouds.'

'As I said, it would not be an easy undertaking, but the rewards are considerable. Once caught, the land will stay solid enough and it will expand to accommodate all who live on it, regardless of their numbers. It is a land of rivers and fields, of tame woods with docile prey, of meadows filled with cattle. It has cities too, empty now but waiting for new inhabitants. The buildings are made of solid marble and the doors of toughest oak. Bridges span rivers filled with fish and eels. There are parks for markets and assignations. In the hinterlands remain little clusters of Fomorians debased from their former greatness but still strong enough to serve as slaves.'

'Why has no one taken it before?' asked the king

Lord Orbsen looked around the company. 'Only the brave and the true at heart can ever take Hy Brazil.' The princess cocked her head to one side and smiled. Her eyes flashed a glittering pale blue that reminded Lord Orbsen of the fragile beauty of mayflies. Never had he seen a mortal creature so heart-achingly beautiful.

'Tell us how it is to be done,' she said.

'Hy Brazil will be visible in three months. It will float across the bay and up the river. By the time it arrives at the great lake it will be as real as your royal hands, princess. Your people must all be landed before noon. Do not delay. Four of your swiftest must run to the corners of the land. In each corner they must drive metal into the ground. As long as the metal remains embedded, the land will remain solid.'

'What form should the metal take?' asked the king.

Lord Orbsen smiled. 'No particular shape is needed. You could use an axe, a hook or a long sharp knife. It does not really matter; anything metal will serve your purpose.'

So it was that in the late summer, as Lord Orbsen had predicted, a great monstrous cloud was seen floating on the waters of the bay. Over the next few weeks the mountain drifted across the bay and into the great river. As it floated up river it began to shrink and solidify. Trees and tall towers could be seen through the mist. Birds and the lowing of cattle could be heard. The people waited, impatient and fearful, on the banks of the lake. Hymns were sung, bodies cleansed, gifts donated to the earth and the water, and boats were made ready to move the entire population on to Hy Brazil.

With first light the exodus began. The first to reach the fabled land were four youths, each carrying a metal-tipped spear. They began to run as swiftly as they could, but none reached his destination. One stopped to marvel at a building made of solid glittering stone; another paused to bathe her feet in a cool gurgling stream; one rested a while in a forest and watched sunlight darting through the silhouettes of trees; one closed his eyes and savoured the breeze as it kissed his cheeks.

Hy Brazil began to dissolve into mist and precipitation. The king proved his worth then, in that moment of calamity, keeping panic at bay with his voice and his willpower. Less than a dozen people drowned. Among the dead, though, was his beautiful daughter. Her name was Gaillimh, which is sometimes pronounced Galway, and from that day the princess's name was evoked by all who travelled on the bay or on the great river. In time, her name would be given to a city as great, if not greater, then any spied on Hy Brazil.

With the failure of the Lord Orbsen's plan, men and women once again turned their attention to the territories of the Tuatha de Danann.

5

PERFECT
WEAPONS

Humans continued to settle on Ireland, coming from north, east and south; constantly rejuvenating the culture, technology and intellectual life of the peoples of the island. Ith was a poet whose family originally came from the land presently known as Spain. In many ways, Ith was the human equivalent of Manannan Mac Lir, being a seeker of knowledge and understanding. It was Ith who dared travel inland, to see for himself the wonders of the domain of the Tuatha de Danann.

Ith was fearful as he began his exploration, but fear soon turned to wonder. In the lands of the Tuatha de Danann the trees were wider and higher than any Ith had ever seen, and the sky overhead was of a blue that left the young man breathless and dizzy. He came to a river so wide he could not see across it, but the waters were so packed with fish that Ith simply walked over their scaly backs. On the other side he saw bulls with horns as sharp as scimitars and great cows with udders dripping cream. Here and there he came across buildings fashioned from stone; massive solid structures topped with turrets and fluttering pennants of many colours.

In the middle of this land he saw three of the great magical lords. They were tall and powerful looking, with skin the lustre

of gold at sunset and long hair the blue-black colour of a crow's wing. Ith crept closer to hear the voices of these masters of time and space, only to discover that the threesome were indulging in a dispute over which lord rightfully owed which piece of land. The pettiness of the discussion so surprised Ith that, without thinking, he stepped out from his hiding place and berated the three beautiful creatures.

'Why are you arguing over who owns what? This land is big enough for everybody and bursting with all a body would need for pleasure or sustenance.' As the three great lords turned to confront the interloper, the anger on each of their faces changed into expressions of abject terror.

Consider for a moment how you would react if you were walking through Galway city and a duck or a dog came up to you and spoke. In a movie it would be a moment for laughter and amazement, but in the real world your guts would shake from the sheer horror and shock of such a thing.

Up until the moment that Ith spoke to them, the Tuatha de Danann had never experienced terror. They had not even known that such a thing existed. Now the three great lords stood paralysed and mute, confronted by the blasphemy of a creature speaking to them. Harnessing their willpower the lords threw off the paralysis and roared out their fear and hatred. With their fists and their feet the lords beat Ith to ground and turned him into a groaning heap of blood and bruises.

Theirs was a hollow victory, however, for not only did Ith not die straight away, but a little shard of doubt had embedded itself deep into the psyche of the Tuatha de Danann that would, ultimately, prove their downfall.

Broken Ith crawled and dragged his way back to the world of men, where he died in the arms of his brother. In his dying delirium, Ith spoke about all wonders he had seen and the savagery he had experienced. In the days and weeks following his burial, news of what Ith had seen and suffered travelled across Ireland. Rage and greed fused together in a fearful alchemy to create a vast army that poured into the realms of the Tuatha de Danann. The rivers and lakes provided the swiftest routes for the invaders. Unprepared, the Tuatha de Danann initially depended on mists, storms and tidal surges to defeat the army, but the Immortals soon rallied and gathered to meet the on-coming enemy.

In the moments before battle was joined, many a man and woman shook with fear and doubt. Opposing them stood the endless ranks of the Tuatha de Danann. The war gear of those great lords and ladies was terrible to behold. The blades of their axes and swords were of a sharpness so keen that when the wind touched them the air split with a high-pitched moan, while sunlight flashed like lightning from their buckles and belts. But the human species has long lived with fear and doubt, and when the cry went up to charge not a one was found wanting.

When battle was joined each side was as savage as the other. Every instrument of death found muscle and bone to bite and tear, and neither army suffered prisoners to live. The wounded were crushed beneath the weight of the combatants, or else drowned in the blood-filled mud. As morning slipped and tripped, screaming and weeping toward noon, exhaustion began to sap the human will. Step by gruesome step the Tuatha de Danann pushed the enemy back. Though they fought on with an animal ferocity, the invaders faced imminent defeat.

The humans ached from lifting the weight of weapons that were now chipped and warped from battle. The Tuatha de Danann, meanwhile, remained as vital and fresh as ever for the weapons they wielded were as light as they were deadly. Yet it was the very perfection of the weaponry of the magical lords that was to prove their undoing. For each weapon of the Tuatha de Danann was truly the Ideal Form of a sword or an axe or a spear. But the Ideal Form is a mirage that can only exist in this world through massive will power and self-belief.

Faced with the undiminishing ferocity and defiance of the humans, one of the magical lords experienced a moment of doubt. Instantly, his sword vanished and he was cut down. Doubt and fear – the gift of the long-dead Ith – swept through the Tuatha de Danann and all their perfect and beautiful weaponry turned to nothing but glittering mist. The men and women fell on them and hewed them down in their thousands. Disarmed, the Tuatha de Danann were no more able to resist the human onslaught than trees the woodman's axe.

It was only exhaustion that prevented the men and woman culling all the Tuatha de Danann. With the coming of evening the victors needed rest. They ordered the broken lords: 'Bury your dead, then leave these lands.' With that, the men and women began the business of carving the great realm into the provinces of Ulster, Meath, Munster and Connaght. All the while the surviving Tuatha de Danann sat or lay on the ground, stupefied with grief and shock.

Among the dead were the kings and queens of the Tuatha de Danann. The wife of Mannanan Mac Lir had likewise been butchered. Grief, however, did not bring unity to the defeated lords. Instead, decimation exacerbated the petty differences and jealousies of the former lords.

As civil war threatened to compound the misery of the surviving Tuatha de Danann, a small group transformed themselves into horses and galloped westward to begin a new life in the Burren. But theirs was to be a temporary respite; with the coming of St Patrick the offspring of these refugees found their way of life threatened. Rather than submit, they leapt from a height known ever since as Aill na Searrach or Aillenasharragh, which translates as the Cliff of the Foals. In the shape of young horses, the Tuatha de Danann tumbled down through salt spray and the screech of fulmars,

kittiwakes and guillemots. When they smashed into the
Atlantic they transformed into the great waves that are nowadays the playthings of surfers from all corners of the world.

After a failed attempt at snatching the kingship of the Tuatha
de Danann, Mannanan Mac Lir was offered the pick of three
sisters to be his new wife. One sister had black hair, one red
and one silver, but his new marriage also ended in sorrow and
eventually Mannanan Mac Lir headed to the west in the guise
of Lord Orbsen. He and his entourage rested at the great lake
where the failed Hy Brazil expedition had taken place. It was
there they were ambushed by Uillinn, grandson of Nuadh,
the former king of the Tuatha de Danann. The battle was
fought on the south-western side of the lake and the land
became known thereafter as Magh Uillinn or Magh Cuillin,
which means the Field of Uillinn. The town and district are
today better known by the anglicised name of Moycullen.
It was at this lake that Lord Orbsen was finally defeated and
killed. The waters took his name and became known as the
Orbsen, the pronunciation of which has changed over the millennia to Orib and then Corrib.

It is only fitting that Lough Corrib provides the water that
brings life, beauty and colour to a bay, county and city named
after the drowned princess whose eyes were the fragile blue of
a mayfly.

QUEEN MEDB AND KING FINNBHEARA

With the defeat of the Tuatha de Danann the peoples of Ireland attempted to replicate the luxurious and golden lifestyle of the former masters of the island. Respect for the former nobles was such that a hundred years after their defeat the first Irish High King, Tigernmas, established a shrine in the north to one of them, Cromm Crúaich. The shrine consisted of a great stone covered in gold, surrounded by twelve lesser silver-clad stones. Cromm Crúaich was flattered and, over the centuries, he would on occasion use his power to increase the yields of crops and cattle in the area.

Tigernmas endeavoured to access greater magical knowledge from Cromm Crúaich, but what he learnt is a matter of conjecture, for the High King and three-quarters of his retainers were never seen again. Those who survived the attempt would not, or could not, speak of what they saw. Clearly, the magic of the other worlds was not to be shared lightly with the short-lived. Without the aid of magic the men and women relied on brawn and brain; as industrious as bees in a hive they laboured long and hard, some using their skills to built forts and fields, others to make music and glittering artefacts. Yet not all got an equal share of the honey.

As embryonic nations evolved on the island, so too did embryonic hierarchies with the lords and ladies at the top enjoying lives graced with song, romance and feasting. Their power was entrenched behind powerful stockades constructed from laws and beautifully crafted genealogies. Their positions of and right to power were promoted by the bards whose work was as exquisite, engaging and enthralling as any modern-day advertising campaign. Yet for all their glory, even the most powerful of men and woman lived with the constant risk of betrayal or battlefield slaughter.

Little evidence remains of the lives of the poor masses but it is worth noting that it was the very fragility and brevity of human life that gave us an awareness and appreciation of being far superior to that of the Immortal Tuatha de Danann. Perhaps this was so with regards to the lives of the poorest members of the nations of Ireland. What can be said with absolute confidence is that of course the poor sang and loved, and ate what food was to hand. Yet their lives were undeniably more brutish than that of the new elites. What little they owned – including their lives – could be easily taken from them in the conflicts between the warlords of Ireland.

Despite their defeat, the remaining Tuatha de Danann still exerted considerable influence on human society. Many of the former lords remained hidden inside hills, caves and the ruins of earlier human habitation or burial – wherein they resumed their lives of luxury, magic and petty jealousies. Whether by choice or sheer happenchance, the interactions of the Immortals impacted on human lives both for good and ill.

Eighteen miles north-north-east of Galway Bay there is a hill called Knockma. From the top of the hill one can look west to Lough Corrib or south to Galway Bay and the Burren. When the Tuatha de Danann ruled Ireland, Knockma was one of the few inland places that humans were allowed to travel to. For it was at Knockma that the granddaughter of Noah was buried in a great stone cairn. Over the millennia the site fell into disrepair, yet it remained a place of pilgrimage for both mortals and Immortals. With the defeat of the Tuatha de Danann, a band of survivors made their home inside the revered hill. One of them, Finnbheara, eventually rose to great prominence and became the overlord of all the surviving Immortals who lived in the area we now know as Connacht.

Much to the annoyance of his wife, Una, Finnbheara had, and continues to have, a great attraction for human women who he would steal away to his palace beneath Knockma. Another form of sport he indulged in was overseeing a great mock battle every year between the Immortals of Connacht and the Immortals of Ulster. If Connacht won then the crops of their human neighbours would be allowed to ripen. If they lost, those same crops would suffer blight and the mortals suffer great hunger.

One of the greatest early human rulers of the west was Medb, who through guile, seduction, murder, quick wits and formidable bravery rose to become Queen of Connacht. Her palace site was Rathcroghan outside Roscommon. Great towering stone walls displayed her power and wealth to friends and foes alike, whilst a cleft in the land known as Owenynagat – the Cave of Cats – served as a portal into the Underworld, wherein it was possible to communicate with gods, demons and the surviving Tuatha de Danann. Medb's seat of power was perfectly balanced for dominion over Connacht and communion with Finnbheara and the hidden Immortals.

What relationship Medb had with Finnbheara is open to dispute. Certainly his mock battles resulting in feasts and famine for mortals would not have worried her too much

– power being the perfect immunity to any local want or worry. Finnbheara's charm, wit and good looks would have stood him in good stead, as would his exalted position. As King of the Connacht Immortals he would have been the perfect match for Medb, Queen of the Connacht mortals.

On the other hand, compared to Finnbheara's magic and longevity, Medb could only have become the lesser partner. Worse still, she would have had to put up with Una, Finnbheara's long-suffering yet ever-loyal Immortal wife. There may have been an attraction between Finnbheara and Medb, even love and friendship, but on balance I think Medb would have rebutted any more passionate propositions from Finnbheara.

Medb was determined to live a life far more exulted than other mortals, where only a few would be her equal and none her master. Anyone who threatened her power was ruthlessly destroyed. She murdered her own sister who had borne a child to the King of Ulster. The child was called Furbaide and years later he would fight with the Ulstermen against Medb's Connacht warriors.

Whilst her life was entangled with the dynastic politicking of Ireland's elite, Medb managed to avoid being entangled with the domestic complications of Finnbheara, King of the Immortals. However, despite her best efforts even Medb was not immune to the machinations and disputes of other members of the Tuatha de Danann.

Long before Medb had been born – perhaps centuries before, if not millennia – two Immortals had become engaged in a dispute that grew steadily more savage as each sought to defeat the other with physical and verbal violence. Both had the power to shapeshift, and down through the centuries they fought with claw, paw, beak and razor-filled jaws, their acrimony growing ever more frenzied.

Then, something unexpected happened. Exhausted and now reduced to the shape of eels, both of the Immortals swam to a different part of Ireland to recuperate and make ready for future warring – each having resolved that the battle could only end with the death and dismemberment of the other. In a state of great fatigue neither of them took much heed of their surroundings, and so it was that one of them was swallowed by a cow belonging to the Daire in Ulster, and the other by a cow in Connacht. There things may have ended, except that the Connacht cow belonged to Queen Medb.

Each of these cows in turn gave birth to a bull that was the reincarnation of one of the wrathful Immortals: the Brown Bull of Ulster and the White Horned Bull of Connacht. The White Horned Bull was horrified to find himself the property of a mortal woman. He left Medb's herd and went to live in the herd belonging to her teenage husband, Prince Ailill, with unfortunate consequences. One evening Medb and her young husband were disputing which of them was superior. To settle the argument they each counted out their possessions. It was then that Medb discovered that Ailill owned a bull of such vigour and power. Determined to match her husband in all things Medb, resolved to get a hold of the Brown Bull of Ulster …

MEDB GOES TO WAR

The Brown Bull lived in the Cooley peninsula on the opposite end of the island, in southern Ulster. Medb sent word to the bull's owner, Dara, that in return for the bull she would let him gain knowledge of her upper thighs. Dara was flattered by the offer, but before any agreement was reached Medb's messenger was overheard mocking Dara, and boasting that if seduction failed he would have suffered a violent death. No proper man would accept such an insult. Dara ended the negotiations and prepared to fight for his property and his honour.

Failing to seduce Dara, Medb set out with a great host of Connacht's finest warriors. Tall and beautiful they were, with glittering weaponry and great banners. Yet their queen believed they would not be needed, for the men of Ulster were under a curse that would see them crippled in labour pains when Ulster was in need of heroes.

As she set out from her palace, Medb found her path blocked by a golden chariot pulled by two great black horses. Balancing on the pole between the horses was a young woman wearing a red cloak with a clasp of gold. In form she was the perfect image of womanly beauty, with long dark eyelashes and ruby lips. Medb knew her at once to be one of the Tuatha de Danann.

'Is that what passes for beauty down below,' she mocked. 'Long legs and eyelashes that yee can scarce see out of.'

'My shape pleases me and my Lord Finnbheara.'

'I'm sure it does; his lordship's taste runs more to the lamb than the ewe.'

'I have a message from my lord,' continued the Immortal woman, but Medb was not yet done talking.

'Where's your belly, girl?' she cried out. 'Where are your hips and your breasts?' With that she patted her own belly and declared, 'I may be too heavy to prance between a couple of ponies my dear, but I have fought and I have f***ed. I have given birth and I have given death. And though I am mortal I am a queen, whereas you are just a messenger girl. So get off yir fancy cart and pay me proper respect.'

The Immortal woman landed on the ground before Medb and gave the slightest of nods. 'My name is Fidelm,' she said. 'You would do well to listen to what I have to say.'

'Finnbheara sent you?'

'He did.'

'Tell him the answer is still no, and it'll remain no until he gets rid of that creature he's married on to.'

Fidelm smiled and her face rippled as if made of water. For the briefest of seconds her features warped into something alien and terrible, then in an instant changed back into the semblance of a woman. 'In my dreams I am visited by visions of the past, the present and the future. When I told Finnbheara of my most recent dream he commanded me to come tell you about it.

'I saw the Queen of Connacht ride out with a great host, each of her warriors bristling with war gear and pride. I saw the Queen of Connacht ride out with a great host to bring sorrow and grief to the people of Ulster. I saw the Queen of Connacht standing in the plains of Ulster and all her fine warriors lain around her smeared with a scarlet silence.

'That was my dream Queen Medb. Take it as you will.'

'It cannot be so. Ulster's warriors are cursed to fail when they are needed most.'

'You forget Cúchulainn, the King of Ulster's nephew. He has a trace of Immortal blood in him and is immune to any curse.'

'Oh, I know of Cúchulainn,' said Medb with a smile. 'A few years ago he came down here looking for adventure and was frightened by the advances of an older woman named Mal. She chased him all along the cliffs on the opposite side of Galway Bay. It was great sport, I hear, with mortals and Immortals placing bets and cheering on the runners. In a state of terror Cúchulainn leapt from the cliffs to a rocky stack. His suitor leapt after him but her limbs were not as lithe as his. Mal fell to her death. The boy kept on running; ran all the way back to Ulster with not a hint of shame on him, bragging to any who would listen that his prowess had saved him from a monstrous hag.

'That is Cúchulainn. A coward. A liar. A man boy with a pathological fear of my sex. I should crush him with my thighs or smother him with one my breasts! I have nothing to fear from him, whilst he has everything to fear from me. I do not need dreams or divination. I simply know it as a fact that I will have the Brown Bull of Ulster and Cúchulainn will suffer gravely if he dare oppose me.'

As it was, both women had spoken the truth. Cúchulainn fought each of Connacht's warriors in single combat. He suffered terrible wounds but succeeded in butchering every man that stood against him. Medb tried to seduce the man-boy, but failed and the slaughter of her warriors went on. With

Cúchulainn distracted, Medb snatched the bull and took it back to her palace. In a field outside the palace the Brown Bull of Ulster saw the White Horned Bull of Connacht. Hatred flared in the breasts of each creature and they resumed their ancient and savage warfare. The Brown Bull triumphed, goring the White Horned Bull to death, and then tearing at its carcass with its horns, hooves and teeth. Exhausted but victorious, the great creature tried to return to Ulster but died of exhaustion.

For all the slaughter and suffering Medb had gained nothing. However, a few years later, using trickery and deceit, she eventually engineered Cúchulainn's death. Outnumbered and with his blood spilling from his body, Cúchulainn tied himself to a post so that he would remain standing as he faced his enemies. Even after his death it was three days before anyone dared approach his corpse. Medb had succeeded in killing Cúchulainn; however, it was the image of Cúchulainn hanging dead from a tree for three days, yet instilling fear into Medb's warriors, that resonated in the hearts of all the island's mortals and Immortals. In time, Cúchulainn's victorious death would be outshone by the image of another man hanging broken from another piece of wood, in the distant land of Judea.

Medb remained Queen of Connacht, yet with so many enemies it was inevitable that she in turn would be murdered.

Her death, though, was not as heroic as Cúchulainn's. Her nephew Furbaide had vowed to avenge the murder of his mother. When he came across his murderous aunt bathing in a pool he hurled a lump of hard cheese at her and so ended the life of Medb, Queen of Connacht.

In her life Medb had, for good or ill, impacted on the lives of countless people, mortal and Immortal; both in her beloved Connacht and far beyond. Her presence had been as huge, as certain and as seemingly indestructible as the waters of Galway Bay or the mountains of Connemara. In the aftermath of her death her powerful lords and ladies competed with one another, each trying to sponsor the greatest tribute, whether by a song or a story or the sacrifice of bulls. Physical monuments were raised in her honour, from the simple Misgaun Medb stone near her palace to the huge artificial hill of Cnoc na Rí in Sligo. Druids speculated on whether she would stay in the Other World or come back and, if so, in the form of what creature? In the more modest huts and fields of the land men, women and children wept or laughed at her passing.

With mortals threatening conflict over where to bury the corpse and who should lead the funeral, Finnbheara quietly slipped into Medb's palace and spirited her corpse away. Out to the fields he took her body, through the Owenynagat and down into the underground passages were no mortal would dare follow. He took the corpse to his own palace beneath Knockma and laid it carefully on a great bed. But try as he might, Finnbheara could not bring life back to Queen Medb's body.

The Last of the Superheroes

Fergus Fionnliath was a Galway chieftain renowned for his contempt for all living creatures. One day a messenger came to him from the great warrior Fionn Mac Cumhaill, captain of the Fianna warriors. Beside the messenger stood a great hound. 'Fionn requests that you look after this bitch until such time as he comes to collect her. Mind her well as she has life growing in her belly.' So it was that Fergus, the hater of all men and beasts, was forced to accommodate another mouth and another heartbeat in his household.

The chieftain's inclination was to beat and starve the creature, but he was afraid of Fionn's wrath. Instead, he treated the bitch with cold respect, which she repaid with warmth and affection. Over the weeks and months Fergus began to show more interest in the dog's welfare. He fed her from his own hand, let her sleep in his own bed chamber, and took her for long walks through the woodlands of Galway and down to the shore, where she ran along the sand and splashed in the glittering waters of Galway Bay. He tended her all through the night and morning of her labour, and was filled with joy when two pups spilled out, blinking and whimpering, into this world.

However, the love that Fergus felt was merely the unforeseen outcome of a jealous Immortal's jest. For the bitch was in truth a great noble woman named Tuiren who had been betrothed to Lollan, a Fianna warrior from Ulster. Prior to the engagement Lollan had a romantic understanding with an Immortal, Uchtdealb of the Fair Breast. It was she who had turned Tuiren into a hound. To compound Tuiren's misery she had then, in the guise of a messenger, given the bitch to Fergus, who she expected would be a most miserable and cruel master.

Tuiren was the aunt of Fionn Mac Cumhaill and when he heard she was missing he threatened Lollan with destruction. Lollan in turn confronted Uchtdealb of the Fair Breast, who confessed her actions but excused them as being the result of her passion for Lollan. Lollan agreed to wed the Immortal if she transformed Tuiren back into her human shape. However, Fionn decided that Tuiren's offspring would not be allowed their true human form. Rather, he ordered that they remain as hounds and that they would live with him.

The hounds were given the names Bran and Sceolan and, as Fionn's loyal companions, they were to become as renowned as any of the Fianna warriors. As to what Tuiren thought of her children being denied both a mother's love and a human form, there is no record.

For all his bravery Fionn, like many an Irishman before and since, had a confused and vexatious relationship with women. He was attracted to feisty, clever, fabulous women, but was perplexed by their refusal to do exactly what Fionn wanted them to do. The gathering of years, grey hairs and wrinkles did not bring him any greater understanding and empathy for the fairer sex. If anything, the disconnection between the reality and Fionn's ideal of femininity became more pronounced with every passing year.

It was in old age that Fionn's trouble with women reached its bitter climax. Like many a noble, the captain of the Fianna understood the need for constantly improving one's position in society, and so it was a moment of great joy when the High King of Ireland, Cormac Mac Art, agreed to Fionn marrying his daughter Grainne, a woman with hair as wild and red as a summer blaze, and with a passion and intellect to match. She agreed to the marriage but at a great celebratory feast her gaze fell on one of Fionn's young warriors, Diarmuid O'Duibhne. And as she looked at him, he turned and looked right back at her.

Later, with the guests drugged or drunk, Grainne and Diarmuid made their escape. And where else would a pair of young lusty miscreants flee to, but the hills and woodlands overlooking Galway Bay? Enraged by the treachery of his betrothed and his vassal, Fionn gathered together a great army of Fianna warriors from across Ireland. Bran and Sceolan too were set on the scent.

On the south side of Galway Bay, in the dark and thick woods of Derry Bo, Diarmuid sought protection from his foster-father, Aengus Og, a lord of the Tuatha de Danann and the brother of Finnbheara, King of the Immortals of Connacht. Wise in the ways and the passions of men, Aengus sought to bring an end to the episode before humiliation and anger turned into bloodshed and sorrow. He briefly succeeded in separating the lovers by magicking Grainne southwards to Shannon River and opened negotiations with Fionn and Cormac Mac Art.

Yet sometimes a story has its own dynamic and, try as they might, participants can do nothing to prevent the outcome. Fionn's fury burned ever brighter. His warriors and even his loyal hounds feared the outcome. In their own ways the men and beasts of Fionn tried to send warnings to Diarmuid, but every such attempt only added kindling to the blaze of their captain's hatred. As for Grainne and Diarmuid, they were reunited and, on the banks of one the rivers feeding into Galway Bay, finally became lovers.

Hunted to the death, the two fled onwards, from the woods in what is today Lawrencetown, westward along the hills and cliffs overlooking the southern shores of Galway Bay. The land before them grew ever narrower until the land was no more and they found themselves facing the dark and restless waters of the Atlantic, stretching on westwards to the end of everything. From this very final fingertip of the known world they looked around, seeking escape. To the south they could see the distant islands off the coast of Kerry, but the lands and waters there

were black with warriors and mercenaries. Looking eastward
to the route they had already travelled, all they could see was a
throng of soldiery, seething like angry ants pouring from their
nest to fight an intruder.

Only northwards, across the stretch of Galway Bay, was
there any hope. The great mountains of Connemara remained,
as yet, untamed by men, being the home of giants, Immortals
and only the rare group of men and women. At the place
known ever since as Diarmuid and Grainne's Leap they made
a desperate jump northwards. But their strength was greatly
reduced and the distance too great; the lovers fell short.

They landed in the middle of Inis Mór, the island that
stretches a third of the way across the opening of Galway Bay.
Inis Mór was the home of a great chief, and the lovers knew it
was only a matter of time before he would send his warriors
to capture them. Near the present-day village of Corruch,
Diarmuid and Grainne made a bed of flatstones and lay
down to watch the sun tumble bleeding into the waters of
the Atlantic. In their hearts they had already accepted this
would be their last evening together. The morrow would
bring separation and death.

But death did not come for them, not yet. For Fionn suddenly called off his hunt. It may have been the wisdom of his
years that finally tempered the Fianna captain's rage, or perhaps
the fear of angering Aengus Og the Immortal foster-father of
Diarmuid, or losing the patronage of Cormac Mac Art the
royal father of Grainne. Perhaps it was enough to have the prey
trapped: killing them would blemish Fionn's reputation; free-
ing them would add lustre.

Grainne and Diarmuid were allowed to live in peace in
Sligo. There they had children and lived a good life. Yet as age
tightened its hold on his limbs, so jealousy tightened its grip

on Fionn's heart. He contrived for Diarmuid to be mortally wounded by a boar, then refused to save him. With the death of her beloved helpmeet, Grainne's spirit was finally tamed and she married Fionn. Yet his victory was short-lived.

It came to pass, not many years later, that Fionn and all his warriors gave battle to a host that outnumbered them sixty to one. Three generations of Fianna fought that day: white-bearded ancients, beautiful long-limbed men and eager smooth-chinned boys. All fell in the slaughter.

In sorrow the Immortals took the heroes' bodies and buried them, and to this day the Immortals have refused to say where the remains of the Fianna lie.

A Terrible
Beauty

Over the millennia the dynamic civilisation on this island evolved and changed, as civilisations must if they are not to suffer atrophy. While much change was of an incremental and gradual nature, 1,600 years ago a new movement convulsed the land with such power and immediacy that within a generation much that had once seemed eternal, deep-rooted and true was broken, lost or reduced to the realm of superstition and children's tales. It was a change that none anticipated; fools and seers alike had no inkling of what was to happen. We that live today have the benefit of hindsight, but it is perhaps best if we begin the account of this change by examining the world that was to be so utterly altered.

In the millennia following the defeat of the Tuatha de Danann a caste of humans emerged who studied the nature of the stars and the seasons, and learned secrets from plants and animals. Some of them became intimate with the Tuatha de Danann, and mastered the art of shape-shifting. These druids knew when crops should be sown and when battles fought. The holy men and women of this order were held in such reverence that they could walk on to a battlefield and order all violence to cease. None would dare violate a druid's command, for fear of magical retribution. Thus the shedding of blood, though copious, was regulated to the chagrin of those hungry for power or fearful of a rival's influence.

The Irish need only look to the squabbles of the contemporary Caesars for proof enough of the dangers of unregulated power. Political struggle in the Roman Empire obliged the devastation of whole continents, the levelling of countless cities and the enslavement of hundreds of thousands, with the fallout vibrating far beyond the spatial and temporal boundaries of the empire. The divinities of the Romans, rather than providing guidance and a staying hand, often delighted in taking sides in the mortal warfare, adding a cosmic dimension to the horror and violence.

As Rome grew ever more powerful, emperors built their courts in those border areas needing most political and military attention. Rome was still revered as the birth place of the empire and the home of some of the greatest Caesars, but politically she had no more importance than a village in the Pyrenees. However, after generations of neglect an emperor once more made Rome the centre of his political ambitions. Like his earlier predecessors, Maxentius took up residency in the eternal city. He added to the capital's architecture, courted the patricians of the senate and paid due homage to the ancient gods.

When his power was threatened, Maxentius went out to do battle with a massive army of battle-hardened legionnaires. The god Hercules lent his support. His voice, bellowing like a bull, resounded over the cheers and whistles of the soldiers.

'I have supported the legitimate authority of men for over a thousand years and am proud to do so again. I am honoured to lend my club to such a gathering of fine fellows. Ah now lads, save your laughter until the enemies of Rome are slaughtered. Then we can all make merry!'

Next morning, in good spirit, Maxentius, Hercules and the men set out to war. The enemy was soon spotted and it was noted that their shields were painted with a strange symbol. Some recognised it as the mark of Christ, a Jew who had died centuries before, broken on a crucifix outside Jerusalem. While some laughed at the enemy, others whispered fearfully the old tales of how the followers of Christ had sung and laughed as they were led to public torture and execution. At Minerva Bridge the two armies met. The blades and spears of the descendants of the Christian martyrs hacked and stabbed with unrelenting ferocity. Maxentius and his great army were cut down. Hercules fled in shame.

The Christian god would no more tolerate other deities than the monarchs of the empire tolerate opposition or dissent. Over the next century the body of a bleeding convict was transformed into both Christ, the glittering symbol of an increasingly tyrannical and inflexible empire, and Christ the hope and salvation of all who suffered. As with all things Roman, the new faith was soon spread beyond the empires borders by trade, fashion, high politics and true devotion.

Even in Ireland, the Christian message slowly but steadily took root, though the believers in Ireland were vastly outnumbered by their pagan compatriots. The pagans were content to have one more god added to the rich and complex pantheon of deities who oversaw every aspect of life and death. The Christians took part in the Immortal festivals and rituals of Irish society, their only qualification being to offer prayers to the one true God. But whilst they offered no homage to other gods, neither did they offer any threat. Indeed, when Palladius was appointed as Ireland's first bishop his task was not to defy the pagan order, but to ensure local Christians did not stray from Papal orthodoxy.

Then something remarkable happened. A joint venture by Irish entrepreneurs succeeded in snatching hundreds of Roman citizens from one of the coastal areas of Britain. Amongst these Christians was a young man called Patrick. The natural order of Patrick's world was, in a shocking instant, overturned. Patrick, a free British Roman of a good Christian family, was reduced to that basest of creatures: a slave in pagan Ireland.

Patrick was sixteen years of age when he was wrenched from his family and nation. Bound in chains, he was sold on to a landowner in the most northern part of the Kingdom of Connacht. Six of the most precious years of Patrick's life, the years that provide the precarious stepping stones between childhood and adulthood, were spent toiling in fields as rains and winds from the Atlantic soaked and froze him. Patrick grew to manhood in Ireland. The fears and desires of that transition took place in a pagan world, his feelings articulated in the language of the Irish; what comfort he received was the comfort of pagan Ireland. In time Patrick came to love the Irish. Only his fervent prayers to the one true God stopped his identity merging fully into the Irish world.

Patrick became intimate with Irish language and society: he observed the power of the druids; the arrogant sway of mortal and Immortal dignitaries. He saw the pilgrims passing on their way to the shrine of Cromm Crúaich, only a day or two's walk away in south Ulster, or setting out for the long journey south-west to Cruachán Aigli, the centre of pagan learning in the kingdom of Connacht. The pilgrims, gay with excitement and anticipation, were dressed in their finest clothes and jewellery. A few had Christian symbols pinned to their cloaks. As these men, women and children passed by Patrick the slave he saw that their faces glowed.

But he knew that it was not joy alone that reddened their cheeks. Shivering with fear, Patrick understood each crimson blush also reflected the flames of Perdition. It was a terrible burden to carry into adulthood – the knowledge that those Patrick had come to love so dearly where all damned to Hell.

In time, Patrick escaped from Ireland. Making his way to France he witnessed scenes of wretchedness and grief as his beloved Roman world suffered one of its periodic bouts of violent instability. He saw that the end days were at hand, and that only by converting the Irish fully to Christianity would he be able to save them from Satan. Yet it was to be many decades before Patrick could return. In that time he deepened his understanding of Christ and His message, while building alliances and contacts that would facilitate his return. Despite, or perhaps because of, ridicule and derision from Britain's Christian elders, Patrick, now grey haired, found money and volunteers for his mission.

One young man was especially welcome. His name was Lugnad, the son of Patrick's sister Limanin. On the mission around Ireland the old man would often come near to being overwhelmed with anger or despair; at other times pride and temptation would threaten him. It was Lugnad, with his steady youthful optimism, who would guide Patrick back to calm reflection. So it was that Lugnad became known as Patrick's navigator.

From the moment he arrived in Ireland Patrick pursued his mission relentlessly. With the arrival of the morning sun, Patrick and his black-cowled followers fell on the drowsy pilgrims at the shrine of Cromm Crúaich. Wielding wooden clubs and crucifixes they smashed the bodies of idols and idolaters.

Hearing the screams of men, women and children, Cromm Crúaich hurried to do battle. He transformed into a monstrous

snake with poison dripping from its teeth. The beast rushed
towards an old man who was shouting out instructions and
encouragement to the invaders. The old man turned around
and laughed at the serpent: 'Don't bother me fairy!' Enraged,
the Immortal snapped open its jaws and swallowed Patrick,
but the evangelist ripped his way through the beast's gut.

Wounded, the Immortal slithered away. Patrick returned to the battle filled with a blinding rage, only to have Lugnad put a hand on his shoulder: 'Enough'. Patrick duly raised his hands and the violence stopped. The pagans who survived were converted en mass and helped their Christian brethren strip the gold and silver from the pagan statues. As prayers of thanks were offered up to God and Christ, Patrick vowed his work was not yet done. 'Cromm Crúaich's shrine is broken. But I will not rest until Cruachán Aigli is conquered.'

In the granite bones of Ireland's hills, atoms shifted imperceptibly as the news of the destruction of Cromm Crúaich's shrine was transmitted across the Island. With one act Patrick altered utterly the realities of this world and worlds beyond. Kings and queens shivered with horror as they contemplated new opportunities for their own advancement or destruction. Even in the realm of infinite possibilities the paths of unborn ideas were realigned by notions of belief and unbelief.

Cromm Crúaich was broken, but Patrick was not yet satisfied.

THE CONQUEST OF CRUACHÁN AIGLI

A shrine to the Immortals had been destroyed but a beacon to the pagan gods remained lit on top of Cruachán Aigli. This too would be defeated. Patrick moved south, but his passage met with fierce political, physical and magical resistance. Time and again the final assault and triumph eluded him, yet every day of his progress contained other countless victories: the winning of innumeral converts to the cause of Christ.

With no neutral ground, mortal men and women were forced to take sides. Having long lived side-by-side, Christians and pagans now found complacency a deadly indulgence. Disruption and fear presaged the imminence of Christ's judgement. Rapture and terror walked hand-in-hand across the hills and valleys of Ireland. Many were saved, but many suffered. Patrick was assailed by weapons temporal and magical, beset by treachery, suffered imprisonment and struggled with needs and desires that daily shook his human frame. Often he came close to succumbing to exhaustion and blackest doubt.

'Thousands have converted,' Lugnad assured his uncle. 'Royal masters and rank beggars have embraced God's light.'

'Only to be attacked by Satan's followers. The lucky have died and been received into heaven. More though have been sold into slavery and prostitution. Of the remainder, fear creates apostasy among their ranks,' Patrick replied.

'Only a few have fallen back into the devil's embrace. Your triumphs and God's promise keep the rest of the flock true.'

'Thank you nephew. As always, your words comfort me and guide me.'

Ever more numbers were converted, with each new soul offering prayers, money and muscle to strengthen the foundation of the Church in Ireland. Miracles became almost common place. In Mayo, Patrick and his followers came across a great mound that was reputed to be the grave of a giant who had died a hundred years previously. As his followers shook in fear, Patrick raised his staff and called the monster from his tomb. The hill shook and a fearsome hand broke out from the top of the hill and pushed the earth away as if it was nothing more than a heavy blanket. The giant sat up and looked down at Patrick and his followers. The creature's face was savage, its eyes red like great vats of blood. The hair on its head was twisted and matted like a forest choked with briars.

'Speak, monster!' demanded Patrick.

'I am not a monster,' replied the creature. 'I was born without the savage inclinations of my kind. Instead, in my life I worked as a cow herd. I protected the creatures of north Mayo, though there was never a man or a child who would not taunt me. And then I died as all mortals die and the grass grew over my chin. But no peace came to me then.'

'What did you see on the other side of the grave?'

'I saw Hell, sir. Saw it and suffered it every hour of every day. The fire blackened my skin and boiled the marrow in my bones. The pain is unending and unendurable. But I thank you sir for giving me this one brief respite.'

'You need not return to Hell. Before this congregation declare your faith in God and the risen Christ and you will be saved.'

This the great creature did. Patrick baptised him and the giant gently lay down again and pulled the soil back over him. 'His soul is in Heaven now,' declared Patrick. 'For the power of the one true God brings salvation not only to the living and those still to be born, but to the dead. Even the monstrous dead can be saved by the true faith.'

In Connacht, Patrick and his retinue travelled with royal permission. The druids, still stunned by the defeat of Cromm Crúaich, stood looking down from the hills at the multitude marching to the next demonstration of Patrick's power. As they marched beneath banners and crosses many of the converts laughed and sang. The druids witnessed many miracles, the most shameful being the raising from the dead of hundreds of pagans so that they might convert to Christianity and return to the grave gladly knowing they were now saved from Hell.

By wing and claw, the gulp of a fish and the snarl of the wolf, the druids sent out word of all they saw. The druids who lived near Galway Bay laboured to build up a stockpile of magic. Volunteers answered the call for ritual sacrifice, but only the purest were chosen to be strangled and placed in the damp peat soil of the vast bogs north and west of Galway Bay.

As the Christians travelled south, the journey became ever more hazardous. Ocean and sky conspired against them, with blasts of ice-shrapnelled rain cutting through the ranks of the devout. Raiding parties snatched stragglers. The Christians struggled to find solace in prayer, but the enemy had placed great war harps on the hills, through which the winds played music of alien and horrific beauty.

Unable to go any further, Patrick halted the procession. While his followers made camp, Patrick and his closest companions went on to confront the pagan magicians. But the Christian God's power was at its thinnest in the northern territories of Lough Corrib. Here the Fir Bolg had once reigned, before they had fallen to the power of the Tuatha de Danann. This had been the domain of Mannanan Mac Lir in the guise of Lord Orbsen, and where Mammanan Mac Lir had returned to the world's waters after Orbsen had been felled by Uillinn. It was now part of the estate of Finnbheara, King of the Connacht Immortals, though he, like many of his race, had been silenced into inaction by the humiliation of Cromm Crúaich.

No report has come down to our age of the confrontation between Patrick and the druids. All that is known for certain is that the saint could not defeat them, and they lacked the power to destroy him and his followers. Instead, the missionaries were taken prisoner and placed on a raft that took them to Inis An Ghaill, the Island of the Strangers, in the north-west of Lough Corrib.

Once ashore, Patrick discovered that the raft remained rooted to the island's shore. He and his companions were now prisoners in pagan-controlled territory. They tried to keep their spirits up, observing to each other that the island had a great covering of trees that provided some shelter from wind and rain, and that the water was filled with fat trout. Yet the trees were not tall enough to block a hazy vision of Cruachán Aigli far to the north-west. The fish were as clever as they were fat, providing only the occasional inadequate meal.

Nonetheless, the evangelists celebrated Christ and defied their captors by beginning the construction of a church on the island. Yet it was long labour and sore. The occasional meal of thin fish soup failed to blunt the edge of their hunger and the trees could not hold back the full force of the violent Atlantic squalls. In the aftermath of the storms, when the sky was a great and flawless blue, the peak of Cruachán Aigli came into sharp and glittering focus. Many of Christ's followers fell ill.

Lugnad's sickness began simply enough. After a day's work clearing roots and topsoil he felt lethargic and weak. He rested the next day, but his strength did not return. Patrick sat with him and they recited prayers together. When the young man shivered with cold, Patrick wrapped his own cloak about him. When he burnt up with a fever, Patrick wiped his face and limbs with a wet cloth. But no improvement came to Lugnad. Soon his mind began to weaken. He stumbled over prayers and became confused as to where he was and whose company he was in.

A week passed. One morning Patrick helped Lugnad sit against a tree. The day was warm. The young man seemed content in an absent way. He lifted a small stone and looked at it. He held it in his left hand and then his right. Smiling, he put the stone down and picked up another. As he watched his nephew, Patrick suddenly remembered him as a child, sitting on his mother's lap gazing at the world with innocent wonder. The young man looked up at his uncle: 'I'm sleepy.' Patrick tried to help his nephew stand but Lugnad could no more stand than a newborn child. Instead, Patrick made a pillow from his cloak and helped his nephew lie down.

The rest of the small group joined Patrick to pray over Lugnad. As they spoke the words of God, creatures stirred. Birds gathered silently in the leafy canopy above; rodents moved in the undergrowth; the water became thick with fish, all looking towards the praying Christians. When Lugnad died the news was flashed instantly to waiting druids and Immortals. They, as well as Patrick's small entourage, wondered what the famed miracle worker would do next.

Patrick bent over the young man's body and raised his arms. His fingertips were lit by a faint sparkle. His companions prayed silently. The old man began to sway gently, his eyes open but glazed as he looked from this world into the next, seeking the soul of his nephew. His fellow Christians knelt in a circle around the tableau of Patrick and his soon-to-be resurrected loved one. All were mute: the devout followers of Christ, the fowl in the trees, the rats in the grass, the fish and eels gawping at the water's edge.

But Patrick shocked them all. With a cry he clenched his fists and stumbled from his nephew's body. 'God forgive me,' he groaned, 'that I should think of tearing our beloved navigator from his final joyous berth.' The old man shuddered as he wept and his companions embraced him with love and tears. Instead of performing a miracle, Lugnad's uncle was the first to begin digging the hole for the young man's body. With every inch dug, Patrick's grief deepened and hardened. Yet it did not destroy him or set him against his followers or his god. Rather, in the days following Lugnad's death Patrick's grief became as a stone against which the blade of his loving faith was made all the sharper and brighter. Dazzled by his rejuvenated belief, the animal spies fled and the spell that bound the raft to the Island of the Strangers was broken.

Lugnad was buried with proper ceremony and a stone in the shape of a tiller placed above his grave. Afterwards, Patrick gave his instructions: 'Stay here and finish building the church. I will return to the mainland and send help. Finally I have the strength to conquer vile Cruachán Aigli.' With that, Patrick stepped on the raft and began his journey north-westward.

That he met no resistance for the greater part of his journey did not assure Patrick. He guessed, rightly, that all that existed in opposition to Christ and His Divine Light would be concentrating their forces on the slopes of that dreaded hill. So it proved: when finally Patrick stepped a foot on the ground before Cruachán Aigli, pagan resistance erupted all around him – before, after, below and above him – with a savage and desperate ferocity. Druids and Immortals cast abominable spells, giants hurled rocks and witches used the subtlest of deceits. Satan and the sea threw in their lot, shrouding the landscape in terrible poisonous vapours. Patrick walked through it all, his love and grief blazing like a fire.

In the higher ramparts of Cruachán Aigli pagan scholars and students trembled behind the walls, whilst young guards gripped their weaponry and vowed to fall in the sacred hill's defence. Through fire and mist the figure of Patrick was glimpsed drawing hourly closer. The terror that assailed him was reflected back a thousand fold on his enemies and spread out north, south, east and west.

The pagans in the upper reaches now trembled and wept with fear as terrible reports and rumour fell amongst them, cold and sharp as winter hail: that every assault on the enemy only made Patrick stronger; beyond Galway Bay the magical horse children of the Tuatha de Danann had been so filled with fear that they had leapt from cliffs into the spitting, roaring Atlantic ocean; the worlds beyond this were in chaos as divinities struggled to agree stratagems, with some vowing eternal war, others vanishing into dreams, a handful advocated switching sides to Christ, if only to avoid warfare without end.

Patrick reached the final ramparts, but met no resistance there. His triumphs had subdued the few pagans that remained behind the stone walls. Soon Patrick was on the peak of the hill; the connecting point between this world and the realms beyond. Determined to cleanse the site of all traces of foul paganism, he vowed to fast there for forty days. The enemies of Christ attempted a final assault, but the great black birds that attacked the praying Patrick were pushed back by a glittering host consisting of angels and souls of the Saved.

Over the days and weeks of his fasting, peace came to Cruachán Aigli, and the witnesses who saw the old man fasting on the hilltop gladly converted to Christ. The site of the evangelist's triumph was soon referred to by the new devout name of Croagh Patrick. On the fortieth day, Patrick, weak from hunger and thirst, stood up. Leaning on his crook he raised his right arm and began to slowly turn in a circle. His gaze and blessing reached across the entire island and soon nearly all the Irish willing embraced God's light.

But Patrick's triumph was not quite complete. As he turned around on the top of Cruachán Aigli he stumbled, and so it was that his holy favour did not quite reach all the island's inhabitants. The unblessed remained resolutely pagan. Was it simply age and battle weariness that caused Patrick to stumble, or had some pagan demon tripped him as a final jest?

Another possibility is that Patrick himself was to blame; that when he fasted he was not humble enough before God's power and grace. When the glittering host had saved him from the shrieking birds it was observed that one of the lights had momentarily alighted beside Patrick, placed a hand on his shoulder and whispered, 'Enough'. But the triumphant Patrick was determined to finish his fast, regardless of any dangers, and in doing so become the equal of Moses, Elijah and Christ.

SATAN'S LAST REDOUBT

The places remaining in the snare of Satan and paganism were said to include Erris in Mayo and Dunquin in Kerry. Of graver consequence was the failure to convert to Christ the three islands separating Galway Bay from the Atlantic. Created millennia ago by two squabbling giants, these islands, Inis Mór, Inis Meáin and Inis Oirr, had long been home to a people whose power and reach were felt not just along the shores of Galway Bay, but further north and south into the kingdoms of Connacht and Munster. Ignorant of his failure, an exhausted Patrick retired northwards to his final rest. The work of eventually breaking paganism in the west of Ireland would be the task of later saints.

Of these, the most important was an Ulsterman: St Enda. The career of this holy man illustrates vividly how Patrick's mission had utterly changed Ireland. If he had lived a generation before Patrick, Enda could well have become a heroic figure in the mould of Cúchulainn. He was a warrior prince, unafraid in war, a skilled and ferocious master of the blade; indifferent to the spatter of gore and brains, the screams of his wounded enemies or imminence of his own violent death.

Feasting, fighting and praise songs of the fili were as important to him as to any of the warriors who lived before Patrick.

Yet Enda was nominally a Christian and his sister, Fanchea, was decidedly so. She founded a convent in Fermanagh and as abbess promised her brother one of her charges in marriage. Enda was now a king in his own right and the need to perpetuate his family dynasty was of greater political consideration than frontline fighting. He agreed to marry and doubtless had many agreeable thoughts about the new direction his life was to take.

He arrived at the convent to find the women there deep in mourning. Fanchea took his arm and walked him through the sound of tearful prayers. 'Your betrothed has died, brother. Come and pay your respects.' So it was that Enda saw his promised future happiness lying still on her bed. For a moment the woman seemed to him beautiful and unblemished in her maidenhood; she seemed to be merely resting. Then in a blink the beauty was gone and all Enda saw was a pale corpse with nuns brushing its hair and washing its hands and feet. The young warrior trembled as he contemplated for the first time in his life the utter finality of death.

'Why would God allow her to die?' he whispered. 'Why would he take such beauty from this world?'

'It is not for us to know the thoughts of God,' replied his sister.

'I am frightened, sister. I do not know where to go or what to do to make sense of this.'

'Put aside your sword and go to Scotland,' she answered.

And so Enda entered the monastery of Whithorn on the most south-western tip of Scotland. He soon became a devout follower of Christ. Over the decades he grew into a respected and influential holy man. His, though, was the grim devotion of a man who had come to accept that God's plan is unknowable; that all men can do is find the strength and courage to walk the path that God set them on.

The path Enda walked eventually took him to the west of Ireland. In the hills, forests and bogs around Galway Bay Christianity was as yet a fragile flower, ever in danger of being crushed by Satan's heavy tread. The populace still revered pagan shrines, druids and Immortals. The Christian leaders of the Gaelic world gave Enda the task of breaking the Beast's last redoubt in Ireland, which was to be found in the Aran Islands.

Enda's royal status ensured his journey was problem free as he travelled from Scotland, down through Antrim and into Connaught. But as he travelled further south he grew more troubled. Whilst Christian worship was evident, everywhere he looked he also witnessed signs of pagan worship. In County Clare the pagan shrines were heaped with offerings of blossoms and bowls of food and drink. Paths, crossroads and river crossings were all polluted with the colour and scent of shameful blasphemy. As Enda travelled down the Atlantic coast he could find no sailor, either pagan or Christian, who would take his fare and transport him to Inis Mór.

As he stood looking at the distant islands, one of the locals was bold enough to mock him: 'I see you are a Christian monk. Are you out to wrestle with the gods then? Ho ho.'

'There is only one God. The rest are demonic imposters.'

'Only one god, is it? I heard you believed in three.'

'The three are one.'

'Ah now, would yir man not get awful confused wondering am I the father the day or the boy or the ghost? Could you imagine him thinking he was the ghost and trying to walk into a wall, only to discover he was the boy and getting a crack on his head like a boiled egg at breakfast? Ho Ho. And his mammy was a virgin I hear? Ah now.'

Enda raised his hand. A thin line of smoke rose from the top of the pagan's head. The man cried out in fear as his eyes rolled upward, his face reddened and his brow beaded with sweat. The smoke thickened and sparks shot out from the pagan's skull.

Groaning in horror, the pagan clutched at his head but then a curious thing happened: rain fell from the sky and doused the flames. The pagan laughed with relief while Enda turned to confront the man who had conjured the rain.

It was another monk. This Brother in Christ was a small man, with a wide smile and twinkling blue eyes. The pagan rubbed his head and spoke to the little monk.

'Did you put out the fire?'

'No,' replied the monk. 'God did.'

'Is your god more powerful than the god of that grim-looking bugger?'

'We serve the same God. Three in One. I could explain it to you if you ever have a moment free.'

'Well it seems to me that you know your god better than this fire-starting fecker. Maybe I will let you explain it all to me. I'd listen to a holy man before I'd bow down to an angry one.'

The monk shook the pagan's hand and arranged a meeting. When the man left, still rubbing his frizzled hair, the monk turned to Enda. 'I am Prince Brecan. My father was baptised by Patrick himself when he was a baby. I've been keeping a look-out for you, my brother.' But Enda did not shake Brecan's hand nor return his smile. He was only interested in one thing.

'How can I persuade anyone to take me over to that great island?'

'Oh, that's easy enough. Stop setting people on fire and try smiling now and then.'

ENDA AND BRECAN

The Aran Islands were once ruled by a great pagan chief named Corban. When rumour came that something untoward had been witnessed in the sea, Corban made ready to hurry out from his fort. As he prepared himself he demanded answers from his retinue, but none of his ministers, warriors, poets or druids would admit to knowing what precisely had been witnessed that morning by the fisherfolk.

'One of you must know. I can see the fear in your eyes. Tell me.'

His wife spoke up: 'A fisherman saw a rock floating on the water.'

'So? Islands move, why cannot rocks?'

'There was a man on it in the garb of a Christian monk.'

Corban laughed. 'Only one, that's barely enough skin to make a belt.'

Corban's wife did not smile. 'This intruder may not be so easy to flay.'

The great chief looked at his wife. She was the perfect companion and match for him in all things: war, politics, art, feasting and, above all else, humour. Now she stood before him, her expression grave. She gripped the long handle of her sword, but her hand trembled and her knuckles were as pale as bone. Corban felt a chill of fear quiver in his belly.

After the druid made a sacrifice and called on the protection of the ancient deities, Corban and his court set off for the coast. They reached their destination that afternoon but did not go directly down on to the sands. Instead, the group waited at a field while Corban took a moment to stroke and admire his twenty beautiful horses. After kissing the brow of a grey stallion, the chief left the horses and walked to the shore. A great gathering of whispering men, women and children were already there. Over their heads could be seen the neighbouring island of Inis Meáin, and beyond it the distant cliffs of the mainland, stark and majestic in the sunlight. As the entourage stepped on to the shore the crowds quickly moved aside. Soon, Corban saw for himself the great dark rock resting on the beach, and before it, a grim-faced monk.

The great chief spoke to the Christian: 'I am Corban, chief of all this land. Climb back on your stony vehicle and leave, whilst you may.'

'I am Enda,' came the reply. 'I care nothing for your position. I once had power and wealth beyond your dreams. I renounced it all for the greater riches of Christ's love. I come today to bring the one and true message of God's light to the people of these islands. So now I ask you to leave. Whilst you may.'

A scarlet rage filled Corban. Raising his war axe he ran at Enda. His warriors raced beside their lord, weapons raised. Enda stepped forward and the warriors suddenly saw their opponent's eyes. Never had they beheld such power and such anger in a man. With a joint cry, Corban's men dropped their armaments and fell onto the sands. But Corban and his wife were not so easily broken. On they came, their rage greater than their terror.

Enda was unconcerned. He held up his arm and pointed over Corban's head. Screams then erupted from the field above the bay.

Corban and his wife turned to see their beautiful horses convulsed with terror. The creatures were leaping, kicking and screaming in torment. Some fell to the ground and rolled as if trying to beat out invisible flames. Then, in an instant, all the beasts turned and galloped towards the sea. The sand burst upwards in a stinging cloud as the creatures thundered across the beach. The sea churned and spat as the creatures rushed into the waves. But the cold water did not end the creatures' torment. They swam further out, still neighing in terror.

'Save my horses!' begged Corban.

'Only if you swear to leave the island,' demanded Enda.

'I swear.'

Enda lifted his arm and the madness left the horses. Calmly, they swam to Inis Meáin. True to his word, Corban, his wife and his court left their homeland on the evening tide and never returned.

Following his victory, Enda began to build the infrastructure that would allow for the worship of the one true God. In contrast to the islanders' former pagan masters, Enda lived an austere and diligent life, and demanded the same from the monks who joined him. Places of worship were built, including the first Irish monastery at Killeaney; rules for monks were enforced; and the new religious rites were propagated. Yet Enda was not a man skilled in the craft of conversion. He was a living exemplar of the terrible and harsh power of his God, but he failed to give proof of his divinity's joy and love. Reluctantly, Enda sent word to the mainland asking for the assistance of monks with a talent for winning over the hearts and minds of pagans.

The new monks were led by one whose humour and joy, it was said, not only won souls to Christ but sent a shiver of fear through the most terrible of demons. Brecan had arrived in Enda's domain.

Soon the laughter and affability of Brecan and his followers brought many of the islanders into the embrace of the Christian faith. They openly discussed their new faith and the joy of conversion, but they also voiced their disdain for the island's grim abbot. Brecan understood, though, that Enda's severity was the hard foundation without which Christ's Church would never be built. Brecan therefore gathered his followers and led them in a procession to Enda's monastery. There he knelt before the abbot and asked if he could become his pupil. When Enda accepted, Brecan turned to his followers and declared, 'Abbot Enda is now my teacher and leader in all things. If you love me you will also commit yourself to be led and taught by our wise and selfless brother.' This the Christians of Aran did. But Enda was still not satisfied.

'Brother Brecan,' he said. 'What rewards we may have earned will be given to us in Heaven, not on earth. However, I would be a weak master if I did not give some recognition for your endeavours. Word has come to me that there are some who believe that I have dominion over too much of this island and that more land should be given to new monks. This is what I propose: a week from today I will say mass here in my monastery, and you shall say mass in yours. When we have finished, you will journey to my monastery, and I to yours. Where we meet will become the border between your territory and mine.'

A week later, the two rivals performed mass in their respective monasteries. Enda's ceremony, as usual, was a slow, stoic and considered affair. Brecan, by contrast, shortened

his mass and was no sooner finished than he climbed on a donkey. His followers cheered in anticipation. Word came to Enda that Brecan was already on his way, but the abbot refused to hasten his mass. Instead, he prayed to God and asked for His assistance.

It was a windy day, but dry and clear, and Brecan's journey should have been easy. But the ground beneath his donkey turned to mud and the creature sank into the brown sludge up to its knees. Brecan's journey stalled. Enda arrived an hour later and asked if Brecan accepted the boundary. Brecan said he did so, at which the mud vanished. Enda was satisfied at his victory, whilst Brecan was amused that he had been defeated by a jest.

From the conflicts and disagreements of these two holy men a perfect synthesis of struggle and joy arose, reflecting the harshness and the beauty of the islands they had brought into God's light. For millennia unmeasured the mass and weight of these islands had mitigated the rage of the ocean beyond Galway Bay. With the arrival of Enda and Brecan, the rocks became the frontline against Satan and his demonic host. The Christian settlement on Aran would be replicated across Ireland and Scotland; the sons of kings and nobles would embrace its teaching and discipline, and pass that knowledge on to the wider world.

INFINITE POSSIBILITIES

The dominance of the mortal princes was – and remains to this day – almost absolute. New secular and religious powers were wielded to reshape society; the druids and their laws were curtailed and eventually extinguished. New codes defining levels of power and powerlessness were created with enough flexibility to allow the very powerful to do as much as they wished. The position of women in society was further restricted. No longer welcome on the battlefield, they were to become passive broodmares for the lords of the land.

The Immortals retreated further into the topography of the land; the caves, glens, riverbanks and forests. Many more left this mortal realm and exist now in perfect abstraction. On occasion they still travel abroad in this world, dispensing gifts or curses depending on their disposition. The older gods remained in Ireland but, following the conquest of Cruachán Aigli, most allied themselves with the new power and earned the titles of saints. Offerings continued at holy wells, stones and rivers but within the parameters of the upstart religion.

Fifteen hundred years after Patrick's triumph, one set of Ireland's princes are still trying to codify, finally and absolutely, the State's control over the wombs of the Mná na hÉireann, whilst their fellow princes ban from the pulpit any who dare to discuss with compassion issues such as female priests and homosexuality. Yet, to the chagrin of these all-too-mortal princes, the people of the island continue to find their own way to joy, creativity and spirituality, often with complete disregard to their self-appointed betters.

This, of course, is very frustrating for Ireland's modern rulers. Yet they only have themselves to blame. From the dazzling fabric of possibilities created by the arrival of Christianity, they choose to see only the one dull and thin piece of yarn that justifies the perverse ideology of a modern State shaped and guided by unelected, unapologetic and unforgiving theologians.

Looked at from another angle, it can be seen that there was much more to the early Christian Church than power and control. The new belief fused local stories and rituals with those from the wider world, adding colour and vibrancy to the individual and collective imagination. Latin, the language of international communication, added new tones and cadences to Irish. Hymns, sculptures and metalwork created a sense of awe and inspiration in all who saw them.

Women played a powerful role in the establishment of the very early Christian Church in Ireland. Enda's sister Fanchea was only one of many women without whom Christianity would not have triumphed in Ireland. In the struggle against paganism there was no room, on either side, for repressed women. With regard to more personal matters, the twenty-first-century ideology that conception equals life would have been regarded by everyone in the early Christian period as weird and as unsettling as the mating rituals of giants. Rather, the hardship of pregnancy was softened and the joy increased by the knowledge that the first twitch of the quickening was proof that a new soul had arrived in woman's belly.

My own children are the inheritors of all these contradictions but are, as yet, blithely indifferent to them. I tell them the simpler versions of the tales that fill the landscape all around us. The stories, though, are restless and ever changing, like the sky over Galway Bay or the lives of Galway's children. Even Yeti Hill lacks certainty. Depending on the season or the weather, paths will change route, distances expand or contract.

Three seasons have gone since I began writing this book. A fourth has begun: Imbolc, when the world opens up to new light and new possibilities. Over this little glint of time many things have happened in my family. My oldest son began school and is now reading, writing and learning different versions of Galway's stories. My youngest son has just turned three. He no longer tumbles and trips as we make our way up Yeti Hill; now he declares himself a mountaineer and sets off with a little blue bag on his back containing vital supplies (a banana and a bottle of water).

For my first walk of the Imbolc I head up the Yeti Hill. My oldest son does not join me, he is at swimming lessons. I am accompanied by the mini mountaineer. At the insistence of my small companion we each hold one end of a long, multi-coloured scarf, this being a vital safety procedure in case any of us should fall. There is a thin smear of frost on the grass and mud beneath our feet, but the sun above has heat in it. It is my son who first notices the smell. 'That is lovely,' he says. I take a sniff. Sure enough there is a faint, warm, softly sweet smell. I look around and see the nearest gorse bushes are already covered in yellow flowers.

As we get nearer to the top of Yeti Hill, we see clues indicating that the yeti may have come into some money. Instead of empty cider cans there are a couple of empty Jameson Whiskey bottles. When we reach the top we stop to peer at moss through a magnifying glass and then look at the landscape all around us. It is one of those clear days when everything can be seen with clarity and precision. I point to the Aran Islands, but my mini mountaineer has more important matters on his mind: 'Where is the creche?'

 'Over there.'

 'Where is the school?'

 'Over there.'

 'Can we stay here a little longer?'

'Of course.'

When we finally get home my son decides he wants to be the storyteller. I sit across from him with my listening face on.

'Once upon a time,' my youngest says, 'St Patrick went to a zoo. He saw some monkeys. They ran away to look for pirates ...'

It is a lovely story he tells, with scary bits and silly bits. And, of course, I am absolutely certain, without a shadow of a doubt, that somewhere in the realms of infinite possibilities a man called St Patrick really is running off to have adventures with monkeys and pirates. I can only hope he remembers to take a little blue bag and a long, multi-coloured scarf, just in case ...

PART TWO:
MODERN TALES

INTRODUCTION TO PART TWO: THE CHANGING CITY

Galway city may seem the quintessential example of an ancient Irish city, but in reality it has only existed for 800 years or so and, for most of that time, the city fathers struggled to maintain its identity as an English colony.

Prior to the coming of the Anglo-Normans, the local Irish had dismissed the location of the future city as nothing more than a stony river, which is one suggested translation of the word *gailiimh*. Other translators point out that the Irish for foreigner is *gall*, thus *gaillimh* means the 'place of the foreigners'. Of course, a certain princess may disagree with both these accounts. It is not only the origin of the city's name that is disputed; far more contentious is the subject of what city stories are worthy of transmitting on to future generations.

A sculpture on the city side of Wolf Tone Bridge commemorates one of the city's international visitors, stating 'Cristofor Colombo found sure signs of land beyond the Atlantic'. No detail is given of what the 'sure signs' were, even though they changed the course of world history. This is perhaps for the best, as the truth is so bizarre that it would cause a rational thinker to doubt if Columbus had ever actually been here.

Columbus arrived in Galway as a visionary, determined to find a way to conquer lands, convert heathens and become rich enough to send gold to ornament the holy city of Jerusalem. Rumour had it that he planned to conquer Hy Brazil or at least use the island as an Atlantic base for further exploration? Certainly, he was constantly on the look-out for clues about the island, its inhabitants and their treasure.

So it was that Columbus was taken along the coast to see a strange discovery. A raft had washed up on the shore. On the raft, wrapped in fine furs, were a dead man and a dead woman. They looked nothing like the people of Galway or indeed Europe. Were they from Hy Brazil? Christopher Columbus examined the corpses and decided they were Chinese. The implication was obvious: that they had travelled from the Orient to Ireland on a mere raft. Thus Columbus need only head west across the Atlantic and he would soon find himself in the lands of spices. This he eventually did, to the sorrow of the peoples and civilisations in the lands we now know as the Americas. As for the dead man and woman, it is now believed that they were Inuits, but their full story remains untold.

Whilst Columbus is celebrated in Galway, other parts of the city's history are simply not talked about. County Galway was one of the areas worst affected by the famine of 1846–49. The work of the historian John Cunningham provides evidence that much of the horror and hypocrisy of those years was played out in the streets of the city. The starving died in the road as their children screamed in hunger; the elites attended charity balls whilst using the catastrophe as an excuse to clear tenants and an opportunity to turn the wretched into forced labour. The story of the famine remains a shameful and unspoken part of Galway's history. Yet those years not only changed the city, county and nation, but had unforseen consequences for the entire world.

In the aftermath of the famine, many fled the west of Ireland for the Americas that Columbus had discovered centuries before. One of the refugees was a woman called Anna Isabel Lynch. Anna settled in Argentina and managed, as all successful migrants must, to make a life for herself. Her descendants remained very aware of their Irish heritage and the continuing struggles in Ireland. Her grandson, Ernesto Lynch Guevara, was particularly aware of his heritage. During his life-long struggle against poverty he would become known by his nickname, 'Che' Guevara. Plans to raise a memorial to this grandson of Galway and its famine have met with constant, and to date successful, resistance.

For the greater part of its existence, Galway city's inhabitants huddled behind walls on the south side of the river. The nearest thing to a suburb was a group of Irish fisherfolk who lived across the river on the shore of Galway Bay. The area where they lived was simply known by the Irish word for shore, *cladach* (now the Claddagh). The group not only brought baskets heaving with fish to the city market, they also brought Irish culture and language. Irish also seeped into the city via farmers, timber merchants and the incursions of the great Gaelic families. Despite the best efforts of its rulers, the city became bi-lingual and has remained so ever since.

However, describing Galway as a bi-lingual city is not strictly accurate. As a trading port medieval Galway was packed with merchants and sailors from the Arctic circle to north Africa, all with their own languages, faiths and customs. All these different voices were heard in the streets, markets and docks of the city. To a visitor walking through medieval Galway, these many voices would seem either a discordant cacophony or evidence of Galway being not just an Irish or English city, but a vibrant metropolitan world city.

Inevitably, the streets behind the walls became too limiting and packed. Bridges were built across the river and the city began to spread and sprawl into Connemara. The Claddagh was only linked to the city by a bridge in the late nineteenth century, perhaps reflecting the disdain of the city elite for a community who played a prominent part in street agitations over the centuries. The original structure was a rickety wooden affair. To add to the dangers of crossing over the bridge, a *gliomach* lived in a hole in the river and would try to snatch away any Claddagh men endeavouring to get into Galway city for a drink, or so said their wives. The bridge was finally replaced in the 1930s by the present Wolfe Tone bridge.

I cannot say for certain that it is the *gliomach*'s hole that features in 'Toby's Wish', the last story in this book. However, it is worth noting that 'Toby's Wish' originates in the Claddagh. To be precise, I heard of the climax of the story from Ellie the musician, who heard it from Paddy the fisherman, whose cousin's friend was there the day the thing that happened happened, as it were. I'll say no more as I don't want to give the story away.

Another Claddagh tale I have included is 'The City beneath the Waves', which is a favourite of my friend Gina who is a very fine example of a Claddagh woman. Whilst it has the appearance of a fantasy story, it carries within it many real and terrifying truths about the power of the sea and its ability at a whim to bless, curse, betray or save those who would dare to harvest it. The story gives further proof that the Claddagh has never existed in romantic isolation from the rest of the world. Thirty years prior to the tale being recorded, a sudden storm in Galway Bay killed nine Claddagh fishermen. The story not only has echoes of older myths, but in parts parallels a horrific event that took place off the coast of Donegal in the 1830s, when an entire Scottish fishing fleet was destroyed by a furious tempest.

The power of the Atlantic weather system is encountered every day in Galway, created by the interplay of sky and ocean. It can in the same day – indeed in the same hour – paint the sky with glittering rainbows or throw down a deluge of rain so thick that day turns to night, only for the wind to blow the clouds away and, in an instant, reveal a sunlit afternoon caped with a vast blue, and cloudless sky. It is this power that has for millennia blessed and cursed the west. The sea can nourish the body with food and provide trade routes, which in turn create exchanges that deepen and widen our intellect and culture. The sea also floods fields and streets, however, tosses fishing trawlers around like trinkets, and makes false and final promises to those hurting in heart and mind. Attempting to make sense of this power has led many to attach gods to each of its many contrary manifestations; others see the contradictions as the workings of one omnipotent god; whilst others see no god, only rain, rain and more bloody rain.

Given the importance of Galway Bay and its surrounding lakes and rivers to the commerce, culture and power struggles in the west, it is inevitable that water features prominently in the two tales of the late medieval period included here. This was a time of great economic expansion, locally and globally. Opportunities for power and wealth became magnified to

unheard-of levels. Yet the vision of success only made failure even more destructive and humbling. With all to play for, men needed to be constantly alert to the machinations of friends and enemies, the whims of lady luck and the compulsions of their own internal passions.

A lake in north Clare is the original home of Connor Quinn's wife in 'Connor Quinn and the Swan Maiden'. It is a love story, but also a warning about the dangers of ambition and pride.

In 'The Mayor's Window' the defining moment of Walter Lynch's life takes place on a ship in the Atlantic. This is a story, like the Columbus one, that is known to every man, woman and child in Galway. There are, though, many different versions of the tale and my account tries to use the best elements of each whilst focusing on the nature of Walter's relationship with his infamous father.

Galway is a city teeming with stories: my notes alone contained summaries of enough tales to fill two books. Despite the evidence to the contrary, one of the most common refrains a storyteller hears is that people are no longer telling stories; that storytelling is a dying art. There can be nothing further from the truth. I have heard the most incredible stories from youngish adults like myself, from the elder community and from children, from people born and raised in Galway, and from people who have settled here either through free choice or desperation. The stories I have heard include magical tales, personal anecdotes and urban legends.

One of the joys of telling stories in Galway schools is that any audience is packed with students whose parents come from many different countries and cultures, and yet the children are all equally passionate about being Irish, and they're all great at telling stories (I suspect this is true of children all over this planet). To begin this collection I decided to pick a story I heard from younger Galwegians. 'The Girl Who Went for the Messages' is very modern, very dark, and perfect for a moody evening. Hopefully it will not only give readers a chill, but convince them that Galwegians are still telling great stories, and doubtless will be telling tales for many more millenia.

Enjoy!

14

THE GIRL WHO WENT FOR THE MESSAGES

Once upon a time there was a little girl called Aisling, who lived in Shantallah in Galway city. She was a golden-haired, eight-year-old child, clever and funny and, like all good children (and indeed like all good adults), she had just enough naughtiness in her to make life interesting.

She lived only five minutes from her school, which was handy because sometimes her mammy would be running late and she would have to see herself home. Her father, meanwhile, worked at the university and usually got home in time for supper at six o'clock. One day, Aisling returned from school to discover a note from her mother on the kitchen table:

> Hi Aisling, I'll be a little late tonight, and I've forgotten to get the messages in. There's a 20 euro note on the mantel piece. Could you go get the messages? We need potatoes, liver, butter, onions, carrots, mixed herbs, a carton of custard, and get yourself a small something as well. Look after the change and come straight home after you've bought everything.

Aisling was pleased to be given such a responsible and grown-up job. She emptied her school bag to make room for all the things she was going to buy, and put the money in the bag's little front zip pocket. With that she went off, fully intending to buy all purchases, be good, and win praise from her mammy. However, just as she left the house she heard the tinkling call of an ice-cream van. Aisling decided it would do no harm to buy the little something for herself before she got the messages. So off she sped in the direction of the bell. She was still full of good intentions, but she was only eight years old – an eight-year-old in charge of a €20 note.

'I'll have a fudge bar,' Aisling said to the man in the van. But when she saw how small the treat was, she decided to have a couple of more things.

'I'll have another bar please, and a packet of crisps – no two, no three packets of crisps – any flavour. No, could you make one prawn cocktail? Do you have rolos? Good. Two packets of those so. No, make that four packets.' And so it went, with her mouth watering and her legs pumping up and down with excitement.

'Are you sure your mammy would want you to have so many sweets?' asked the man.

'Oh, it's fine. We're having a party and my mother has put me in charge of catering. But I think that will do for now.' With that, Aisling handed over her money and stuffed the goodies into her bag. As she took the change she realised how little there was left to buy food for supper. But it would be too shameful to give the sweeties back.

Aisling walked through Shantallah until she came to the little park that contained the famous Sliding Rock. It was a good place for a troubled soul to sit down and think. The Sliding Rock was famous around the entire world. Everybody knew that a priest was buried under the rock, or it might have been a nun, and that they returned to life at night to scare children and steal pizzas off them. Well, so her friends said. But Aisling also knew it was famous for another reason. Long ago, long before the houses were built, the great Daniel O'Connell stood up on the rock in front of half a million people and demanded Catholic Emancipation. Aisling ate a bag of crisps and tried to imagine such a massive crowd of people. It was a sunny day and she began to relax, and as she relaxed so she began to form a plan – not as big or important a plan as Daniel O'Connell's, but a plan nonetheless.

Off she went to the Westside shopping centre. She had a skip in her step but she remembered to be very careful crossing all the roads. In the shops she set about buying the food. Her plan was to buy a little of everything and then either say she'd been short changed, or the prices had all gone up, or a big girl had stolen the change. That part of the plan was not quite firmed up, but the main thing was she could still buy enough for the evening meal.

So she bought a small bag of potatoes instead of a large bag, and did the same with the carrots and onions. There was only one size of custard but if you bought two you would get an extra one for free. Aisling added three cartons of custard to her shopping basket and a packet of butter.

'Where can I get liver?' she asked the lad at the checkout.

'Either over at the meat counter or up at the hospital!'

Aisling did not laugh. She paid for the messages, took her change and sternly said thank you to the boy.

At the meat counter the smiling butcher asked her how much liver she needed. As he spoke he scooped up a handful of the slippery brown viscera, scarlet blood dripping through his gloved fingers.

'How much would three helpings be?'

'Three euro.'

Aisling counted out her remaining coins. 'I only have 89 cents.'

'Well, I could give you one helping for that.'

'But I need three. I get my pocket money on Saturday. I could pay you then. Liver and onions is my daddy's favourite food. So I really need the liver now. Please.'

'Sorry love. I can only give you one.'

Aisling bought one helping, and then ran out the shopping centre, tears welling in her eyes. She was not sure what to do. Her plan had been so simple and yet it had not worked. It was not fair. She had let her mammy down and her daddy would only get a miniscule helping of his favourite food. Aisling bit into a bar of chocolate and thought for a bit. 'Daniel O Connell didn't let anything stop him. I won't either,' she decided, jumping up. As she walked to the road she looked to her left and smiled. 'Yes!' Across the road and ten minutes' walk away was the back of the hospital. Aisling, a resourceful girl, had another plan – even better than the last one.

The little girl with her bag filled with sweets, vegetables and a little bit of animal innards walked down to the back entrance of the hospital, navigated her way round parked cars, numerous little huts and buildings, and came to the front entrance. The front desk was busy and the receptionist looked stressed.

'I'm so sorry to bother you,' said Aisling so sweetly and politely, 'I know you are very busy, but I'm not sure where to go for my appointment.'

Her smile would have melted the coldest of hearts and, sure enough, the receptionist smiled back and asked for her letter.

'Oh, I forgot it.' Aisling said, squeezing a tear from her eyes, 'Oh, this is terrible. I have a class project to do. I so wanted to come top of the class and I was doing it on a big difficult subject and a doctor said he would meet me. But I've forgot the letter and now I'll fail.'

'What was the project on, love?'

'Organ transplants, and the doctor said he would take me up to where the organs for transplanting are kept. Though he promised I did not need to look at them if I thought they would be too gory. But he would tell me all about it. But he's not here and I've not got a letter and, and ...' Aisling hiccupped and sniffed.

A crowd had now gathered around her, all with letters and confused faces; all wanted to know where they should go and how to get there. The receptionist took a letter from the nearest hand, then looked at Aisling again.

'The transplant doctors are always a bit forgetful. Head over to the corridor and take the lift to the top. He should be up there in the Organ Transplant Wing. If not, I'll keep an eye out for him down here.'

Aisling ran off, smiling and delighted. She quickly found her way to the elevator and made her way up to the top floor. When she stepped out she looked around, but there was no one to be seen. She walked down a pale green corridor until she came to a door with a sign on it that stated 'Transplant Organs. Qualified Staff Only Beyond This Point'. Aisling took a deep breath, rubbed her head, bit her lip and then pushed the door open.

She had expected a big room full of scientific instruments and bits of bodies lying about, but instead the room was small and sparse, containing only shelves on which metal flasks of various sizes stood. A little notice had instructions written on it: all equipment was to be left plugged in and switched on and should only be handled sparingly and with great care. Each flask had two little lights. If the red light was on it indicated that the flask was empty; if the green light was lit it showed that an organ was inside the flask awaiting transplantation.

Most of the flasks seemed to be empty, but the green light glowed on four of them. Each of these had a label on the front explaining its contents. The first contained a pancreas; the next a small intestine; the third a stomach. The fourth contained a liver. In her excitement, Aisling almost dropped the flask. She held it tightly to her chest while her shaking fear subsided. 'It's okay. Just need to stay calm.' She unplugged the flask and placed it carefully on the floor. It was easy to open: the top just screwed off like a regular flask.

A freezing white breath rose from the open mouth of the flask. Aisling wafted it aside and look inside. She could see tightly packed iced cubes and a glint of pale brown. She reached in to grab the liver but quickly snatched her hand back. The inside of the flask was so intensely cold it felt as if she were trying to put her hand through a fire. Aisling, resourceful as ever, sat back and considered. She rummaged in her school bag and found an empty crisp bag. Holding the bag with one hand, she tipped the flask with the other. Ice cubes spilled out and soon the liver was at the flask opening. There it waited, fleshy and pale, looking like a tongue in an open mouth. When the organ quivered Aisling squealed with fear.

'It's only my hand, shaking the flask. That's all. The liver's not alive. It's not going to jump out or shout for help or anything.'

Aisling, brave as a princess confronting a dragon, placed the crisp bag before the liver and carefully tipped the flask. The organ slipped out and flopped into the bag. She folded the bag over and shoved it in her pocket. Her fear of failure or of being caught had vanished, only to be replaced by another worry. She was a good girl, and she had managed to get all the messages so her mammy could cook the supper. However, stealing was naughty, even if it was for a good reason.

The chill from the icy puddle was seeping into Aisling's bones, but she did not leave the room. After putting the flask back on its shelf, she took a pen and a piece of paper from her bag. Her brow creased as she tried to remember what she had learned in school about writing proper letters. After a moment of intense thought, she began her letter.

She wrote her letter properly enough by placing her address in the top right-hand corner. She stopped, thought for a moment, then wrote:

Dear Sir or Madam

I have borrowed the liver. I am very sorry but I really needed it for my daddy. To pay for it I have left a big bar of chocolate which I hope you will enjoy.

    If you ever need anything from me, please do not hesitate to ask.

Yours sincerely

Aisling

The schoolgirl folded her very well-crafted letter and propped it against the flask. She put her bag on, patted her pocket and left the room. Fifteen minutes later she was home, panting and laughing with delight at her adventure.

The secret to being a successful criminal is not letting inner guilt reveal itself through words or deeds. Sadly, Aisling had much to learn on this score. Her mother's suspicions were first aroused when, walking into the kitchen, she beheld a most remarkable sight. Aisling was sitting at the table, chopping onions. On the table were two pots, one filled with freshly scrubbed potatoes, the other with peeled carrots.

'Why thank you, Aisling, this is a wonderful surprise.'

'Well, I know how hard you work mammy, so I thought I'd help you get daddy's favourite meal ready.' With which words her mother became convinced that something was wrong.

'Did you get the messages okay?'

'Yes mammy. Only the butcher was short of liver so I only managed to get two helpings. They're in the fridge.'

'And was there enough change left over to get a treat?'

'Well, mammy.' But Aisling never uttered her planned excuses. Suddenly, overcome with guilt, she blurted out: 'Oh mammy, I did a terrible thing. I went to the ice-cream van and I bought so many sweets that I nearly didn't have money left over. So I could only afford a little bit of potatoes and carrots and liver and, oh, please don't be angry.'

'How many sweets did you buy?'

'Lots. Sorry. But I've got all the veg ready and I am really sorry.'

'What did you do with the change?'

'Oh mammy, there is no money left over.'

'Twenty euro. You blew twenty bloody euro?'

Tears poured from Aisling's eyes as her mother slapped the table. A minute passed as daughter wept and mother muttered softly to herself. Jesus was mentioned in the woman's whispers, but the other words were of a more profane nature. Eventually, her mammy calmed herself down, hugged Aisling and put everything right. The sweets would count as a month's worth of pre-bought treats. Aisling promised to do the shopping better next time, and mammy thanked her for preparing the meal. With balance restored, Aisling went to her room to do homework whilst her mammy began cooking.

Soon the house filled with a mouth-watering aroma. Whilst the onions fried slowly in butter, the carrots and potatoes were chopped and put on to boil. Daddy came home just after this with a kiss and a delighted cry of 'Liver, my favourite!'. He took the little white bag from the fridge and looked at the soft slippery flesh inside: 'It looks lovely and fresh.' His wife took the bag and told him to go get changed. She too was impressed at the quality of the liver, in particular the smaller, pinker-looking one. She quickly chopped the livers and added them to the golden onions. There was blood inside the bag and on the chopping board. She tipped this into the mix as well, then added salt, pepper and, her secret ingredient, a glass of red wine.

Father's mouth filled with saliva and his belly grumbled appreciatively. Upstairs, across the landing, the warm sweet smell drifted into Aisling room, exciting both hunger and nausea in the girl. As the scent grew thicker and richer she felt she was choking. When her father came in to tell her that supper was ready, he found Aisling leaning out the open bedroom window. Her hands gripped the windowsill as she gulped down great gasps of fresh air. When she turned around her father was startled to see her face was white with a greenish sheen to it.

'Sorry daddy. I ate too many sweets today. I'm too sick to eat.'

'Okay love. Do you want water, anything?'

'No, thank you. Nothing. And I don't want any food kept. I just want to go to bed.'

'Okay. I'll check on you later.'

Daddy went downstairs and told his wife about Aisling's illness. 'It'll be her conscience,' laughed mammy, taking a sip of wine. 'She went mad with a twenty euros today.' They sat at the table and exchanged news. It being an adult-only meal, their talk was bolder than usual and the wine flowed with greater energy and volume. 'This meal is incredible,' said daddy. He stared at the meat impaled on the end of his fork. 'Seriously, I have never tasted liver as light and succulent as this.' Mammy raised a glass in the general direction of their daughter's bedroom: '*Maith thu*, Aisling.'

After the meal, daddy washed up while mammy took a plate of mashed potatoes and gravy up to Aisling.

'Thanks mammy, I feel a little better now.'

'Do you want to come down watch some telly?'

'No. I'll just stay up and read for a bit or play some games.'

'Don't stay on the computer too long. You still have homework to do.'

'I've done my homework already.'

'Good girl. Can I get you anything else?'

'Milk and a hug, please.'

'Of course.'

The earth spun on, the sun rolled down the sky. Night came on, neon-lit, as the family slept. Then, in the middle of the night, Aisling's mother woke up. She put a hand on her husband's shoulder, gave him a good shake and whispered, 'Did you hear a sound?'

Daddy sat up in the bed, groggy from food, wine and romance. 'I don't hear anything.'

'There's someone in the house. I'm sure of it.' Mammy tightened her grip, transmitting a subtle buzz of panic to her husband.

'I locked up, I'm sure.'

'Well, go look, husband!'

'You heard the noise. You go look.'

'We'll go together.'

So husband and wife rolled back the blankets and put on slippers and robes. They walked through the gloom to the door. Mammy put on the light and gripped the door nob.

'Ready?' she whispered. Daddy's belly quivered with fear, but he managed to nod. Mammy opened the door wide. Daddy stumbled into the hall, switched on the light and breathed out.

'See. There is nobody here.'

The two adults stood on the landing, feeling foolish and relieved. It was then they heard a beep coming from their daughter's room. Mammy laughed. 'It's only Aisling and her bloody computer.' As she spoke they heard another beep. It was a small sound but precise and clinically so. She looked at her husband. 'It's too late for games,' she said crossly.

Daddy nodded in agreement, 'She should be in bed at this hour.'

They walked across the landing and opened the door of Aisling's room, and stepped into a scene of horror.

Mother's reaction was instantaneous. Her mind, refusing utterly to engage with the scene before her, shut down. Her legs buckled and she flopped to the floor like a broken manikin.

Father did not faint. He stood there staring, unable to make sense of what he saw. Images floated by like a blurry dream. Colours registered: violent white and shocking scarlet. But there was a disconnection between colours and images. A weight thudded against his leg. He looked down at his wife. He heard a beep. As he turned towards the sound, images and colours began to coalesce.

Someone had placed a second bed in his daughter's room. A man lay on it. There was an oxygen mask on his face. Taped to his chest were wires. The wires came out from a little box that beeped. A little part of daddy's mind clung to the belief that this was a dream or a joke or maybe, given it was summertime, a piece of guerilla theatre. Three figures stood beside this bed. They wore rubber gloves, face masks and white smocks spattered with red dots. One held a sharp scalpel and one a long syringe. The third held something small, pink and slippery looking. In an instant daddy knew exactly what the object was. As he began to howl in horror and grief, the figure with the syringe stepped forward and stuck a needle in his arm.

As he crumpled to the ground, he saw Aisling lying on her bed, grey and motionless. A terrible wound was in her side; the skin parted like a gaping mouth, blood still dripping out from her lifeless body.

15

CONNOR QUINN AND THE SWAN MAIDEN

One day, as the light was fading, Connor Quinn walked the length of his estate. It was a pleasant walk along the edge of a large lake. When he came to the ancient ruins of his family's ancestral home, he sat down and looked at the lake stretching away from him. A gentle breeze cooled him. The sun was low on the horizon and the rippling water glowed red and gold. As he rested he saw three swans moving gently on the water. Each bird was attired in feathers as white and dazzling as midnight stars and they moved with a grace and nobility that showed their superiority to any of nature's other creations.

As the creatures drew closer to the shore, Connor was touched by a deep and terrible melancholy. Compared to the perfection and contentment of the three birds his struggle for wealth and power seemed pitiful. His whole life had been dedicated to bringing renewed honour and status to his family, but suddenly he understood that his name and his history had no more importance than a speck of dust in a giant's eye, or a grain of sand in the hand of God. The swans, on the other hand, seemed to Connor to exist with a complete disregard for the limits of time and space.

The swans continued to move across the lake, drawing nearer to the shore where Connor sat. The young man wiped his eyes and carefully hid himself behind a broken wall. Sending a wish and a prayer out to the infinite, he peered over the ruin and saw, to his delight, that the swans were now stepping onto the grassy bank some thirty or forty feet away. One of the creatures nodded its head and stretched out its great white wings. Connor was horrified to see hands suddenly sprout out from the middle of the creature. With a sickening rip the hands tore the swan open and out stepped a young woman. The swan's form was now nothing more than a beautiful cloak, which the woman folded with great care and placed on a rock at the water edge.

The two other swans likewise opened up to reveal two more women, each of whom also folded her robe and placed it on the rock. The three women walked away from the lake until they came to a flat piece of ground only a few yards in front of Connor. Each of the women was similar in appearance, with copper skin, thick black hair and dark eyes. Even the curve of breasts and the musculature of limbs were replicated in each of the three. The only difference seemed to be in age, and so Connor knew that the three were sisters.

Before the gaze of the astonished young man the three swan women formed a small circle, facing outwards and clasping each other's hands. First they dipped and curtsied, then stood upright and stretched towards the red and purple sky. It seemed to Connor that some invisible force was connecting the three for they moved with such perfect synchronicity: when one bowed, her sisters did the same; when one bent a knee, whilst stretching her arms wide, the movement was perfectly and instantly replicated by her two companions.

Then, with a gleeful yell, each released her grip and leapt forward. Mesmerised, Connor watched the youngest of the

sisters stomp the grass with her naked feet, then slap her hands on the naked flesh of her thighs and belly. Her sisters too were yelling and jumping in a frenzy, their skin glowing scarlet in the dying sun's light, their hair a wild raven-black aurora. As they spun and screeched, sweat spun off the tips of their fingers and the point of their breasts. Their musky scent filled Connor's nostrils and mouth, choking him and filling him with terror, lust and white-hot sparks that blazed through his groin and his gut until in a sudden rush of madness, he scrambled over the rock and ran roaring towards the women.

With a yelp the maidens ran to the lake. The older two grabbed hold of their cloaks and, in an instance, transformed into swans. The younger sister tripped only a few feet from the rock. She cried out for help but her two sisters beat their great white wings and took flight. Connor jumped over the fallen woman and snatched her swan cloak. With that he turned and walked all the length of the lake back to his own grand house. Not once did he turn around, for he knew the young woman had no option but to follow him. When he arrived home he went into his hall and walked towards the great hearth were logs blazed and spat. Holding the cloak before the fire he turned and faced the swan maiden.

There she stood in that great hall, with its tapestries and furnishings from all the corners of the world, with a hundred candles glittering and the great oak beams overhead. There she stood naked and defenceless, but no tears spilled from her dark eyes. Instead she stood proud and wary, looking first at her cloak and then directly at Connor.

'I know what you want, Connor Quinn,' she said, 'And I will be your wife, your willing wife, but only if you do two things for me. You must give up gambling, for it is a childish folly and I have sworn never to become the bedmate of a fool or a boy. And you must never bring a member of the O'Brien family into this house, for they are an enemy to me and mine.'

Connor rang for a servant and asked for a Bible to be brought for himself and clothing for the swan maiden. He swore then to keep his side of the bargain and smiled as he made his pledge. Gambling was a pastime he could easily forgo, and the O'Brien family and Connor's family had for many centuries been the bitterest of foes.

So it was that Connor Quinn married the swan maiden. After they were wed Connor gave his wife her own chamber that opened onto the great hall. It was only then that she let him know her human name: Beatrice. The chamber contained everything a woman would need for comfort: a great bed, soft chairs, a box of sewing material and a rope to summon a servant at any time of the day or night. There was a large window that looked over the lake, and hanging from a hook on the wall was the beautiful swan cloak. Connor kept to his side of the bargain and his wife to hers, and the cloak remained untouched as the months and the years went by.

Many sages have written, sung and extolled the innumerable virtues that go towards making a marriage successful. None, though, have ever mentioned the benefits of mistrust and uncertainty. Yet it was these two attributes that helped bring closeness between Connor and his wife. Having committed to sharing a life together, neither was sure what to do next. In the weeks following their wedding the two kept a resentful distance from the other. Each assigned malign motives and desires to the other that, with every day, became blacker in the imagination. When finally they confronted each other it was only to discover that their fears lacked any foundations.

From that moment they were both more careful and attentive of the other's needs. One morning Connor came into the hall to find his table had not been set for breakfast. A servant was called for and an explanation demanded. 'The mistress of the house asked that we lay the master's meal out in her chamber', explained the serving girl.

Connor went in to his wife's chamber and there they both sat facing each other, a small table between them. They ate a little, they drank a little, and said not a word during the meal. With the meal over Connor attempted to break the uncomfortable silence.

'If you wish, I could have food put out by the lake for your two sisters.'

'That pair! They've food enough. What they need is a stick across their backs.'

'Why?'

'You know why. When I needed them most they fled.'

'Would you rather return to them?'

'Oh Connor, do you want rid of me now?'

'No. But I would not have it said that I forced you to live a life filled with sorrow.'

'And I would not have it said that I broke a pledge.'

'So you will stay.'

'I will.'

'In which case,' declared Connor with a grin, 'I will get a stout stick to teach your sisters a lesson.'

Beatrice smiled and shook her head. 'Oh dear husband, I pity the man who ever tried to hurt me or mine.' She put her hand on his. Her skin was soft and her grip firm. She kissed Connor on the cheek. 'If you are free this evening, perhaps you would care to join me for supper.' Sparks shot through Connor's belly, and he laughed at his fortune and his folly.

'Maybe,' he said and kissed his wife's hand.

A year after they were wed husband and wife were sat at the breakfast table. The previous twelve months had seen a change in Connor's fortune. Investments yielded stunning returns, merchants up in Galway City begged his patronage, and powerful men took account of his views on the great politics of the state. Good fortune seeped into the very soil he walked on and the air that he breathed. His lake was packed with large and sweet-tasting fish, the trees appeared wider and their foliage thicker. There was less sickness amongst his tenants and none could recall when last his crops had been bigger and more abundant.

'Who knows,' said Connor, 'maybe one day I could regain all the land my family once controlled here in Munster and up in Connacht. It would only be fitting; Queen Medb was my ancestor after all.'

'That would explain your nose,' said Beatrice. 'I thought I had seen its like before.'

'Dear wife, you must be very distracted. Queen Medb lived a thousand years ago.'

'Was it that long ago? How strange.'

Connor took a bite of meat. His wife frowned, then addressed her husband.

'Husband, I have unexpected news that terrifies me almost as much as it fills me with joy. I have a child in my belly.'

The birth, when it came six months later, was a long and agonising enterprise. After twelve hours a trembling serving girl was sent with a message to Connor as he paced the great hall. 'The mistress fears she is dying, and begs you give her a good and Christian burial.'

'Can I see her? Should I call for her sisters?'

The serving girl curtsied and returned to her mistress's chamber. The door had no sooner shut than a shriek of pain and rage resounded through the building. The serving girl stepped back into the hall. 'Begging your pardon, master, but the mistress says that you need not attend to her yet, nor send for her sisters.'

'What were her exact words,' demanded Connor? The girl's face reddened and she shook like the final leaf on a tree in an autumn storm.

'Come,' said Connor gently, 'A penny for an honest answer.'

'Well, begging your pardon, master but the mistress only shook her head when I asked if you could see her. When I mentioned calling for her sisters, her reply was more loud and fulsome.'

'Her exact words, please.'

'To be exact, she said, "My sisters can go to hell, and take the fool that dares consider inviting them".' Quickly the girl added, 'The midwife asked me to say that the mistress's response shows her strength and resilience.'

Connor laughed in relief and handed the girl a coin.

Beatrice endured ten more hours of pain, stabbing like a blade as her body pushed and kneaded life into the child. Ten more hours she suffered as none of her kind had ever suffered before. Ten more hours of arduous agonising journeying into motherhood and womanhood, with death and life alike attending her, each offering peace or punishment as the mood took them. At last there was a final scarlet stab between her legs and, suddenly, Beatrice was free of weight and of worry as the wailing child was placed on her sweat-soaked breast.

'Tell my husband he has a son.'

It is a rare achievement to balance ambition and contentment, yet for seven years Connor managed to do precisely that. Eighteen months after the birth of his son, Beatrice bore him a daughter. Now Connor had a child to inherit his estate and a child to offer in political marriage. Yet political calculation did not blunt the affection Connor felt for Beatrice and his children. As his income grew, so the great hall filled with the sound of merriment as the children crawled, walked and then ran circles around parents and servants.

During the summer the family walked the length of lake, taking food and drink to the ancient ruins. At first Connor was afraid to return to those antique stones. 'It is important,' explained Beatrice, 'that we make that spot ours. My sisters must understand they have no ownership over any of this land. It belongs to you, my husband, and you alone.'

The swans were seen on the first family expedition. They floated on the waters, white and magnificent, paralleling the progress of the little group. The oldest child had stopped to look at them. They stopped too, to stare at him with their black eyes. Beatrice had grabbed the boy's shoulder and hissed at the birds. They flapped their wings and took flight. It would be many years before the creatures returned.

No matter how many times they visited the broken ruins, Connor always began the picnic with the same words.

'Here is where I first met your mother,' he would explain to his children. 'She was dancing.' Each time he said this he sounded astonished as if only realising for the first time how blessed he was.

Beatrice, for her part, would grasp her husband's hand and laugh, 'Oh, *grá mo chroí.*'

Exactly seven years after he had first seen his future wife dancing with her sisters on the banks of the lake, Connor kissed Beatrice and his children goodbye and promised to bring them a little something when he returned from his trip in a few days time. It was the season for horse racing, a time when the powerful met to shake hands, slap backs, cut deals and quietly or boldly – depending on the disposition of the men involved – shape the politic and commerce of the land. Connor never missed a festival and though he now never enjoyed a flutter he sponsored a number of celebrated races.

As well as the sports on the racetrack a racing festival was (and is to this day) the arena in which all men, from the meanest labourer to the wealthiest banker, could observe whose influence was waxing fat and full and whose influence was on the wane.

Connor's prestige was clearly on the rise; he was a figure to be observed, pointed at and, if lucky, win a shake of the hand from. With the last of the day's meetings finished, the great men of the west retired to a tavern to eat, drink and assess what hand Fortune had dealt to each of the day's players. Connor's successes that day included an amiable discussion about the sacred and societal importance of marriage with Mayor Lynch of Galway who, after many childless years, had recently been blessed with a son, Walter.

As the night wore on ever more men packed into the tavern. Candles spluttered in the hot gloom, casting a smoky light. The air was thick with the reek of horses and earth, of onions and stewed meat. The festive banter was punctuated with laughter, shouts and the occasional thumping of the table. In the midst of all this a cheery voice called out, 'Is Connor Quinn so elevated above us he cannot enjoy a bet on the horses like other mortal men?'

Connor replied, equally merry, 'A drink for that man to dip his tongue in.' But his heckler was not satisfied with the tankard that was placed in front of him.

'In all seriousness, Connor Quinn, your behaviour is troubling. If the greater can't spare a coin on chance, why should the lesser. If we all followed your example no risks would ever be taken. Nothing ventured, as they say, and nothing gained. Soon it would all be stagnation from Ballyhannon to Belmullet.'

'Oh, I have taken many a risk in my life,' replied Connor, 'and made many a gain, as many of these gentlemen will testify. I have more than enough coin and would not take the chance for gain away from others. Indeed, happy as I am in life I now extend a drink to everyone in this fine place!'

'And doubtless you would ask us all to raise a glass to the health and happiness of you and your good estate.'

'Not at all. I need no more joy and wellbeing. As for my estate, how could it be any better? The trees on my land are bigger than houses. So many fish are packed into my lake that you could walk across their backs and never wet the soles of your feet. My home is filled with tapestries from the Indus and beyond, and furnishing inlaid with gold and ivory. My son is as handsome as a prince, my daughter as happy as a princess, and my wife as good and as fair as an angel from heaven.'

The stranger stood up with a suddenness that knocked his fellow imbibers sideways.

'Gentleman, listen to the great Connor Quinn. The way he talks you would think he was one with God and our saviour. Maybe he should be given an ould bit of mackerel to turn it into a feast for thousands. Or perhaps we could ask him to turn a basin of dishwater into a casket of finest Spanish wine.'

No one laughed. Not a voice was raised in agreement or dissent. Every man there, from the labourer to the overseas trader, remained silent as Connor stood up and carefully gave his reply.

'Stranger, if you are as honest a man as you are foul-mouthed, you will come to my estate now and see for yourself that I have spoken the truth. You will then return to this place and tell these gentlemen that every word I spoke was free of falsehood and exaggeration.'

'I accept the challenge. What's more, I will add another round of drinks for these good witnesses.' With that the stranger took out a purse and spilled gold coin on to a plate. 'This should keep everyone in good form until I return.'

Connor and the stranger got up on their horses. As they galloped across the country trees grabbed at their hats and hedgerows at their boots. Above them the moon and stars shook and shone as white and bright as swan feathers. It was only when they arrived at Connor's estate that the two riders allowed their creatures some rest. Trotting along a laneway, Connor gestured to the trees on either side. 'Big as houses, as I said. And look over there, observe the lake. You can see the backs of the fish glinting in the moonlight.'

When they came to his great home, Connor invited the stranger to lay a hand on the stonework and take a look at the turrets and carved figures leering down from above. 'It would take a morning to walk around this building, and a hundred years of to knock it down.' The stranger nodded but said not a word.

Inside, Connor showed the stranger his great furnishings inlaid with precious metals and jewels, the tapestries from the furthest corners of the known world, the hearth open like a vast mouth in which a great tongue of yellow and red flame licked and lolled. 'The fire and the candles are always lit, no matter the hour or the season,' boasted Connor Quinn. The stranger nodded and finally spoke.

'I admit to being impressed. You spoke the truth, my friend.'

Connor gestured to the two chairs by the fire. Between the chairs was a small ornate table, on which Connor placed two glasses and a decanter of whiskey.

'I am glad to win your approval; you will of course transmit your opinions to the witnesses.'

'Of course,' said the stranger with a smile. 'I give my word as a high-ranking member of the ancient and noble O'Brien family.'

At this, Connor trembled with dread. He tried to speak, but his mouth was dry and his tongue swollen and heavy. He struggled to breathe, yet forced himself to fill the glasses. With the taste of the whiskey he snapped back into a semblance of composure. Another drink was poured. With a merry 'Sláinte!' Connor clinked his glass against O'Brien's. All was not lost; his wife and his children were asleep in their chamber. He need only remove his unwelcome guest as quickly as possible and all would be well.

'It is well that an O'Brien has visited my home. Our families have spilled too much blood and anger over the centuries. Let us drink to our mutual good fortune and continuing prosperity. Let us also commit ourselves to meeting again at a more hospitable hour.'

Connor stood but the O'Brien remained in his chair. He stretched out his legs, took a sip of his whiskey and gazed at the fire. Finally he turned to look up at Connor.

'Well, I guess I should take my leave now. There is a tavern filled with gentlemen who are awaiting my honest assessment of your possessions. I will, on my word as a gentlemen and an O'Brien, tell them that everything you said was true. That your trees are as big as houses; your lake packed with fish a man could walk across the backs of. I will tell them about your rich furnishings and delightful tapestries. I will tell them about the blaze in your hearth and the glitter of your candles. But I will also make sure to tell them, on my word as a gentleman and an O'Brien, that yours Connor Quinn is the worst hospitality in the whole of Ireland. Never before has my mouth suffered such a brief acquaintance with another man's *uisce beatha.*'

Connor sat down again. A true gentleman, he would rather a knife in the belly than such an indictment. Wounds can be recovered from and scars displayed with pride, but a reputation for frugalness in a host is an injury as evil as it is fatal.

'Ah now O'Brien, you need only have said that you had time enough for a proper welcoming. There is more whiskey in the cabinet over there and some cheese and fruit, though it would be my pleasure to wake the kitchen and have a more substantive supper prepared.'

'Whiskey, cheese and fruit sounds a grand enough supper. *Go raibh maith agat.*'

The two men ate and drank and drank and ate. Connor kept his voice low and was grateful when the O'Brien followed his example. The whiskey, as whiskey does, induced conviviality between the two men. Connor wondered why he had not met his guest before, and O'Brien explained that he had been raised in the court of England.

'I have returned to oversee my family's commission to control piracy in Galway Bay. My approach is more one of regulation that eradication. But even in England I heard news of your own improved standing in life. What is the secret to your success?'

'A good and loving marriage,' declared Connor. '*Ni ceart go cur le cheile!*'

O'Brien raised his glass in agreement, 'It is very true. Only unity brings strength. But I see you glancing towards that door there. Is that where your wife rests?'

'My wife and my two children.'

'Well,' whispered the O'Brien. 'Let's finish the evening soon, and finish it as strong friends.' He took a packet of cards from his pocket. 'Let us play a quiet game Connor Quinn, before I go out to tell the world of your honesty and good fortune?'

The guest dealt the cards and the host happily picked up his hand. They played in silence, the only sound in the vastness of the hall the slurp of lips imbibing, the clink of glasses touching, the sigh and snap of cards playing. Connor won a couple of hands; the O'Brien likewise. After a while the O'Brien spoke softly.

'What is a game between friends without a little flutter…?' Connor agreed and the game began in earnest.

Both gentlemen remained polite and outwardly affable, but the game had changed into a competition as savage as any battle or politicking. At first the men were equally matched in intellect and stamina, but as the whiskey brought weariness and confusion to Connor, the O'Brien became ever more focused and full of vitality. The hours crawled by as Connor first lost his wealth, then his land, then his beautiful furnishings and tapestries. In a last desperate bid to win it all back Connor lost his grand house.

The O'Brien sat back in his chair and raised a glass to his stupefied opponent. Connor was numbed and shocked at the massive and utter reversal of his fortune. When he heard a door slam he leapt up in terror, grabbed a hold of the O'Brien and

dragged him across the hall. 'To hell with hospitality!' he roared
and threw his enemy out into the cold pre-dawn darkness.

He walked back into the hall, placed a hand on the door of
his wife's chamber. A great fearful melancholy echoed through
his belly and heart. Wiping away tears, he opened the door.

His wife was standing by the open window. Outside the sky
was grey and purple. The two children stood in front of their
mother. Behind Beatrice stood two woman with feathery capes
draped over their shoulders. Connor reached out to his wife,
but one of her sisters opened her mouth in a wide terrible gri-
mace and hissed. The other sister took the swan robe from the
hook it had rested on untouched for seven years. She placed it
on Beatrice's shoulders.

'You have no more hold on me,' wept Connor's wife. Before
his eyes she and her sisters began to mutate into great white
birds. As Beatrice's arms transformed into wings she touched
their children and they too began to change.

One by one the five creatures leapt up to the window and
flew off into the blood red sky of the new morning. And that
was the very final ruin of Connor Quinn.

16

THE MAYOR'S WINDOW

As merchant, mayor and judge of Galway city, James Lynch FitzStephen was unflinching in pursuing his own interests and destroying those of his opponents, potential opponents and any allies who became too influential in the politics and commerce of the west. His was a position of almost unassailable power and few dared defy him.

When his son Walter was born, Mayor Lynch looked upon the child as he would any other investment. Harshness and an unbending will would surely generate a profitable return. Children, however, are not insensate like granite, marble or caskets of wine. And while infants are amiable to bribes and responsive to threats, they lack the necessary appreciation of power that businessmen and politicians have, the result being that their response to inducements and intimidation can be unpredictable.

As Walter grew, his father's frustration became deeper and sharper. Try as he might, the man that ruled one of Europe's greatest cities could not establish control over his own nursery. Sanctions, whether violent or more subtle – the destruction of a favourite toy, say – only made the child more wayward. Denied a foundation of love and warmth, Walter became as uncontrollable as the Connacht weather – interspersing sunshine with savage storms. With every year that passed the child became more ungovernable. When fourteen years of age, the heir to the Lynch fortune found friendship among a gang made up of the delinquent younger sons of the great merchant and aristocrat families, both English and Gaelic. The boys' entertainment included rampaging through Galway at night committing acts of vandalism and moral outrage, and freely using words and phrases from the barbaric vocabulary of the natives.

One summer, when the lad was sixteen years of age, Mayor Lynch sent word that his son should come to his business quarters as a matter of urgency. The mayor owned a property in Galway City's Market Street that towered five floors high. The topmost room of the house contained a tall window. The frame of the window opened inwards like a door and by fastening it to a metal bracket could be secured in this position, allowing Mayor Lynch to stand on the sill. From there he could look down on the rabble below and, equally important, the rabble could look up and see the full form of their superior from the flash of his boot buckles up to his fine red cap.

Walter arrived late. He had drunk and danced late into the previous night. His skin was grey and his lips moved as he struggled with the nausea in his throat. He sat down without asking permission. Mayor Lynch ignored the insult. They were seated at a small mahogany tabled inlaid with pearl and rubies. Mayor lynch placed a casket before the boy. When he spoke to Walter, his tone was warm, his body language relaxed. 'Please open the box.'

Walter did so and for a moment his heart and his breath stopped. The box was brimming with golden coins, each reflecting the candlelight. Walter's father continued to speak, the reasonableness of his voice more unnerving that the words uttered: 'I have a task for you. If you are not up to the task then I will give you half of these coins and send you on your way. You will no longer be my son, but the little fortune you take with should be enough to set you up in life of prudence or debauchery, as you will.

'If you accept the task, then there is a possibility of my retaining you as my son and heir. If you succeed, you will bring honour to yourself and the potential for even greater wealth.'

'What if I accept the task but fail in carrying it out?'

'Drinking, whoring and gambling are weak and pathetic pastimes, Walter, but worse, far worse, is failing in business. If you accept the task I set you but fail to bring it to a successful conclusion you will be stripped of title, income, clothing and thrown naked into the street.'

'So I can refuse to accept the task and be rewarded with a little gold, or accept the task and risk losing everything?'

'That is so.'

'And what is the task?'

'I will only tell you after you have made a decision.'

The boy looked at the gold; the mayor looked towards the long window. The mayor had failed to understand Walter as a child, but Walter was now a young man, and Lynch had never yet failed in weighing up a man. Sure enough, Walter pushed the casket back towards his father: 'I'll take the task, whatever it is.'

The mayor looked back to his son and said, 'I would like you to prepare two ships, travel to Spain and bring back the finest wine at the cheapest price.' He pushed the small fortune back to his son. 'There is enough in the box to complete the task. You may keep a quarter of whatever is left over as well as all the profit after the wine is sold in Ireland.' The mayor did not remind his son of the consequence of failure. In all the years he had lived the mayor never felt the need to repeat a threat to anyone. He simply took his son's hand, shook it and left the room.

Left alone with the gold the youth felt a sudden need to drink wine, play cards and taste a woman's lips. He looked from the gold to the door, but knew his flight would be witnessed by his father or his lackeys. He turned to the window and blinked. Before him he saw the silhouette of someone crouched down. Slowly the shaded figure stood up, shaking as if from the some great physical or emotional effort. Walter managed to stand and the vision instantly vanished. The young man laughed and rubbed his head. 'Sweet Jesus, I'll be seeing fairies next.'

To Walter's delight he found the task of organising and planning his voyage as fascinating as any card game or dare: one eye had to remain firmly on the task at hand, whilst the other kept a look out for those variables and happen-chances that can change a game in an instance. Two ships were requisitioned, and two crews employed, all of whom – sailors, officers, carpenters, butchers – needed to be thoroughly assessed for experience and character. Requisitions included hens for eggs, biscuits, dry meat, tea, water, lemons, cloth, canvas, nails, saws, buckets, splinters, rum and bandages. Walter also bought wool and hides to sell on in Malaga. By late summer the ships and men were ready. On a fresh and favourable morning, Walter set out for Spain.

Youthful confidence and an inability to contemplate failure meant Walter was sure of his success in Spain. Arriving in the port of Malaga, he entertained the merchants of the city on board his ship. As the Irish sailors sang, danced and played whistles and drums, the men of the city ate a fine meal. The meat, wine, fruit, even the cutlery and crockery, had all been purchased in the local market. With goodwill abounding, the boy then gave each of his guests a little silver token. The small gifts – letter openers, ink pots and the like – were given by way of thanking the men for their company and reminding them who they were dealing with. For on each little trinket was stamped the Lynch family crest.

'My father has given me a task, gentlemen, which I hope one of you will be kind enough to aid me in. I am to fill my ships with your country's finest wine for the lowest price possible.' With this statement Walter gave an incredulous laugh. The merchants thumped the table in front of them. Some nodded their heads in appreciation of a good joke; others smiled and shook their heads in bemused wonderment. Walter raised his glass and cried out, 'Viva la Reina!' The merchants cheered. Soon enough stars were glittering above and the entrepreneurs stepped merrily ashore and climbed up into waiting carriages.

The next day a number of messages were delivered to Walter. Most merchants declined his offer; some expressed interest but in a manner that was not to the young man's taste. Some were too florid, others promised bargains that seem too extravagant. One card, though, struck a chord. There was no need for the service of the translator, as the correspondent had written in good plain English: 'Thank you for your gracious meal Master Lynch. I may be able to supply you with excellent wine. My price will not be the cheapest but it will be good. I will also consider giving you a considerable discount if you do a favour for me.' The card was signed simply 'Felipe'.

Walter sent a gracious reply and was rewarded with an invitation to dine that evening. A golden carriage pulled by four fine Arabian horses collected Walter at sunset and conveyed him to a mansion in the middle of the city. A servant took Walter's coat and hat; another offered him a flute of champagne; whilst a third asked Walter to follow him. They walked along a

corridor, the walls of which were made of a pale blue-veined marble that recalled the skin of the round-breasted woman who had first introduced Walter to sensual pleasure. Every couple of yards or so silver and bronze statues of pagan gods frolicked precariously on ebony plinths. A partially opened door offered Walter a glimpse of a room filled with glittering candles and dancers moving slow and gentle as a morning tide.

At the end of the corridor was a door painted crimson and gold. The servant stopped and bowed to Walter, who pushed the door open. Beyond was a small plain room. The only illumination came from a pair of candles in the middle of small table. At the far side of the table sat a man Walter recognised as one of the city's merchant. 'Excuse me if I do not stand, I am not as agile as I once was. I am Felipe. May I call you Walter? Good. Title and ceremony can be as bothersome as rheumatics and age. Please sit. My fellow merchants were impressed by their visit to your ship. Most, though, expressed concern at your age and your conceit. I mean no disrespect. I merely want to give you an honest account of their opinions. Many of my colleagues would seek to trick you into buying poor product, which is of course their due right. I, on the other hand, am as old as I am rich. Years ago, decades in fact, I used to cringe when I recalled the things I said and did when I was a youth, but now in my infirmity I see things differently. I have come to understand that I would not have my present wealth and comfort if it was not for the opinionated and over-confident youth that I once was. I see you are smiling. That is good. Let us eat and then we can discuss business.'

The meal, of a plain and easily digestible nature, was eaten in silence. Felipe was a slow and careful eater. Only when the last dish was cleared away did he speak again. 'I have a nephew, Rafa, young like yourself – but still adverse to responsibilities. Would you be interested in being a companion to him? It would be of great benefit to him and his family if you were to show him how youthful vibrancy can be turned into great and profitable deeds. Take him on your ship. Show him how the right lad can command men and make money. In return, I will fill your ships with the finest wine.'

'With a discount?'

'But of course. However, you will have to be patient. The fiesta starts tomorrow, so it may be a week or so before I can procure the wine for you. In the meantime, enjoy Malaga. The fiesta is a wonderful time, though I would advise you to place guards on your ships. Sailors can very easily go astray. As for Rafa, his family lives out in the country. I can arrange for him to be here after the fiesta, if you agree to take him.'

Walter did agree and was rewarded with a small glass of the wine, as dark as midnight dreams and as smooth on the tongue as a maiden's lips. 'This is but a small sample,' explained Felipe with a smile, 'of the wine I shall be purchasing for you. A month from now you will be unloading it in Galway, with Rafa's assistance.'

Walter returned to the docks that evening. A guard was ordered for the two ships. However, the captain of Walter's ship advised too tight a clampdown could easily lead to riotous disruption, the only cure for which would be the hanging of two or three men. Instead, Walter's crew were set the task of organising their own festival night, for which they had to scrub and clean the ships and repair the sails, as well as make decorations, rehearse songs and sketches. In keeping with the festivities a tot of grog was given to every man and boy in the evening, whilst each morning began with a short mass before breakfast.

With harmony on board, Walter rewarded himself by going ashore to experience the festival first hand. Walter was a man who worked hard and fairly to bring his ambitions to fruition, but as he walked ever deeper into Malaga scents and sounds crashed like waves around him. The young man's outer maturity and sense of right and wrong suddenly had all the fragility of sails in a storm; sails that snap from their bounds and, attached only by one frail rope, flap loudly and aimlessly on the mast, leaving a ship floundering without direction.

Walter the man quickly devolved into Walter the youth who walked, laughed, stopped, stared, gawped, ran and danced his way through the streets of Malaga. He felt the madness building inside him, as if his skin was a sack filled with cats and snakes all twisting, hissing, clawing and screeching. He could feel his blood spitting and bubbling in his veins, his limbs twitching in expectation, his mouth salivating, his hands gripping.

Days and sensations blurred into one another. He stumbled into lamp-lit midnight revelries, where the rich and wretched together danced, embraced and swapped goblets of wine; he scrambled in the mud for the coins cascading from a hurtling carriage; he laughed and roared at grotesque pantomimes; and he was stunned into a terrified silence by a solemn procession of robed and masked figures carrying icons and relics. As he choked on the cloying reek of incense a woman put her hand on his and the touch of her skin was as terrible as it was joyous.

Walter ran then, weeping, collapsed in a church, and stared up at an icon of Mary the Queen of the Universe. The young man shook as he prayed, and slowly his youthful madness shrank and shrivelled till it was nothing more than a pale ghost snared in the back of Walter's skull. He returned midweek to the ship, just as the sailors were beginning their own festival. He quickly washed and shaved then went on deck to begin the sailors' celebrations by opening a keg of rum. With the men still cheering, Walter retired to his quarters.

He lay down and eased into a dreamless sleep, undisturbed by the sounds of the men as they sang, danced jigs (the dancers included three woman who had been smuggled on board), gave speeches, told tall tales and feasted on tender meat and crisp vegetables, followed by fresh fruit and another tot of rum. The festivities climaxed with a joyful drunken brawl, which was quickly suppressed by the guards' clubs. No further discipline was required.

Walter and his men awoke the next day head-sore but ready for work. Wool and hides were unloaded on to the quay and the ship was prepared for its homeward journey. A day after the festival ended wagons trundled on to the dock. They were accompanied by a young lad on a fine grey horse. Walter stood on the dock and waited while the youth dismounted and talked quickly to the men unloading barrels from the wagons. Satisfied that work was progressing, the lad walked over to Walter.

'I am Rafa,' he declared with a bow. 'My uncle has sent me with your wine, which is in those barrels. There are also a dozen bottles, which Uncle Felipe has added as a gift. My uncle says I must obey you in all things and that in doing so I will become mature and more businesslike.' The Spaniard laughed with joy. Walter, touched by the lad's merriment, gladly shook his hand. The sun was bright, the breeze strong, the tide slowly rising, and Walter was delighted by the prospect of such an amiable companion for the journey home.

The day continued in its happy hung-over way. The wool and hides were sold for good profit. The barrels loaded without any spillage. Walter locked the bottles in his quarters. Six of the bottles he would give to St Nicholas' church in Galway and six he would give to Mayor Lynch, God and his father both deserving thanks. With the turning of the tide the two great ships sailed the ebbing waters out from the docks. Weather depending, the ships would be docking in Galway in a matter of weeks.

The peace of the Mediterranean allowed Walter time to show his companion around the ship and tell him how the trip had been organised. Yet as they explored the ship they noticed the mood of the crew was sullen. Walter called over the ship's captain. 'Tell me, what troubles the men? Speak freely.'

'Well sir,' explained the captain, 'none of us has ever been on a journey so free of mishap. It's unnatural and wrong. Not so much as a sprained wrist or a man falling from the rigging. The men are worried that perhaps Fortune is saving us from a lot of little troubles so as she can punish us with one big one.'

'Why would Fortune wish to punish us?'

'To remind us, sir, of how unimportant we are in the vast scheme of things.'

Once out in the Atlantic, however, the mood of the crew rose with the ocean's rolling swells. The men's good humour induced a wonderful conviviality on board. As Walter and Rafa

walked the deck they shared accounts of the many and varied
youthful indiscretions each had committed.

Three days out on the Atlantic and a sudden storm blow-
ing out from the south shook the last idle worries from the
men. The captain and crew of each ship deftly negotiated the
great and terrifying mountains of water that, every moment,
threatened to toss men heavenward or plunge them down to
hell. For two days the storm roared: winds screaming like a
banshee's warning, rain pounding like hammers, waves smashing into the ship's frame with the power of cannon shot.

In Walter's quarters the two young men held each other
tight, cleaned the vomit from each others' clothes and roared
in terror and exhilaration as the room bucked and spun violently. Inside the locked cupboard the twelve bottles of wine
rattled and banged like bones trying to escape from a crypt.
And all the while beyond the fragile panels of the cabin, sky
and sea, and all the elements between strived to destroy the
ships.

Yet after two days the raging tempest stopped as instantly
as it had begun. With a few last derisory gusts the storm
ceased. The men were red eyed from exhaustion and soaked
to the skin. Some had suffered broken limbs and one had been
blinded by a splinter from a snapped spar. But not a man had
been lost and, as the sky cleared and the water calmed, a great
sense of elation filled the ships.

Walter and Rafa stumbled on deck and looked at the men
in wonder. For forty-eight hours the fate of all aboard had
tipped between life and a cold and sodden grave. Yet from
their smiles and laughter one would have thought the sailors
were merely sportsmen; a team of hurlers, perhaps, who being
two points down in the last seconds of a match, had scored a
winning point.

'The men should be rewarded,' Walter suggested to the captain.

'I've thanked the men already. That will suffice for now. They have a good energy on them. Any distraction will break the pace.'

'Should they not rest?'

'Ah, they're as giddy as boys now. I would suggest keeping the sport going. The storm blew well for us, now I think its time to keep the speed up.'

'A race to Galway?'

'Indeed, with a prize for the winning crew.'

Wind and waves were now in harmony, and the two ships clipped along with firstly one in the front, then the other. Nor did night bring any respite as the competing crews sought advantage over each other. Not a breeze could wander abroad without a sail being set up to catch it. Every curse and every prayer uttered ended with the same exhortation: 'Faster lads, faster!'

Tragedy came to Walter and Rafa, however, on a night when the ships sped with swollen sails. The race was in to its third evening and the young men's ship had fallen a half-mile behind its competitor. The two lads were standing at the rear of the ship, neither one speaking, each looking at the vast and alien vista that bound them on all sides. The milky wave arched overhead, its innumerable specks of silver emphasising the cold and lifeless depth of the cosmos. The stars' reflections were caught in the net of the sea, blurring the boundary between earthly and cosmic oceans. It was only the ship's blue glowing wake that gave proof that it and its crew still moved through mortal waves on a mortal world.

'It is too beautiful,' said Rafa. 'Let's us go in to the warmth and light.'

The two men stepped through the door and shut it against infinity's terrible beauty. Walter lit candles, while Rafa carved up the supper.

'Should I light more candles?' asked Walter.

'No, the light is perfect. As is the meat. Come friend, let's fill our bellies and relax.'

The lads sat down and ate the succulent meat, but neither could shake off the chill that had crawled beneath their clothes, seeped through their skin and settled in the marrow of their bones. Walter lifted a decanter and poured out a weak sub-standard wine that he had brought with him from Galway. As he sipped he remembered the smooth richness of the wine he had tasted in Malaga.

'What are you smiling about?' asked Rafa as he carved another slice of meat.

'Oh I was amused by the irony of our situation. Here we are on a ship filled to bursting with Spain's finest wine and we are drinking pink piss!'

Rafa paused in his task, his hand still gripping the knife handle. One half of the knife's blade was deep inside the meat. The exposed half held Walter's candlelit reflection.

'My uncle Felipe is a great man and an honest man,' the young Spaniard said carefully. 'However, I can make no such guarantee that the middle men who bought the wine on his behalf were as equally true.'

'In which case, we as merchants owe it to our future clients to check the quality of the wine.'

'Precisely. There are twelve bottles in there. We need only open one. Just to make sure.'

'It is the only sensible course, Rafa. I suggest you stop carving and start rinsing this muck from the glasses, while I open a bottle.'

The wine was opened, the glasses filled. The lads sipped the dark and smooth liquid as the ship sailed through the light of stars quick and dead, and the green-blue sparks of agitated phytoplankton. The lads sat relaxed in the room, not the slightest tremor disturbed the wine in their glasses, and a lazy warmth dripped slowly into their bones and sinews.

'The top of the bottle was grand,' declared one.

'Let's check the middle so,' added the other.

Soon the lads were chatting and laughing. As more wine was poured, the room filled with the scent of summer flowers and citrus fruits, adding a bucolic flavour to their pleasure. Their talk wandered and wound easily over a range of subjects: the racing of the ships, the vastness of the ocean, the quirks of sailors, tales of home and history, of family and wealth and plans for the glittering future. As they spoke, they drank. As they drank, the lads became ever more in tune with each other's loquaciousness; each knowing when to listen, when to speak, and when to interrupt with a joke or an ejaculation of wonderment or faux shock.

Inevitably the talk turned – as talk always does when young men are at ease and ruddy with drink and happiness – to the subject of the fairer sex.

'Tell me about the women of Galway?' asked Rafa, his words a smidgeon slurred and his brow furrowed from the mental effort of making coherent conversation.

'Oh, they are right bonny girls – *go hálainn* indeed!'

Walter raised his glass to the beauty of west coast women. Rafa raised his too and, confused but happy, declared, 'A toast to the boney girls of Galway who go Holland!'

'Oh I'm sure they do,' spluttered Walter. 'And the men of Holland would be delighted to welcome them.'

'Make them go Spain!' laughed Rafa.

'Oh, Spain has no need of Irish women.' Now Walter's brow was furrowed and his expression serious as he struggled to explain himself clearly. 'The ladies of Spain are just as beautiful as Galway girls and ten times more elegant. I danced with one at the fiesta, her dress was cut low and her black eyes held a twinkle and a promise of ... a kiss!'

Both lads laughed. The glasses clinked, drops of dark wine spilled. 'Oh, my country women can do more than kiss,' declared Rafa, passion lending coherence to his thoughts.

'And what do they do?' asked Walter.

'What would you like a lady of Malaga to do?'

'Oh, many things.'

'Tell me.'

Walter described in detail what he would ask a Spanish woman to do. At first Rafa clapped in delight and appreciation, and adding sound effects and helpful suggestions. But soon he became quiet and still, his eyes closed as the images Walter wove filled his mind and his gut with sparkling sparking images of limbs and sweat and darkness exposed. The more Walter spoke, the more his descriptions strayed into darker and more explicit imaginings. Rafa opened his eyes in horror, but though he stared hard and wide-eyed at the candles, he could not break free of the awful words that held him rigid in his chair. Walter paused to take a sip of wine. Grinning, he asked Rafa, 'Do you have a sister?'

'*Diablo*!' The young Spaniard staggered from his seat and grabbed hold of Walter. With their limbs softened by drink, the blows each aimed at the other landed weakly. Like clowns in a circus they stumbled about the room, throwing punches that often missed, attempting kicks that unbalanced the kicker. After the briefest brawl, as is often the case with drunken lads, fierce anger would surely have given way to frustration and frustration to laughter. But even as a sense of the ridiculous began to bubble beneath Walter's rage he fell against the small dining table. He flung out a hand to brace himself only to have his fingers connect with the handle of the carving knife.

The weight, the glint and the perfect form of the instrument so overpowered Walter that it seemed as if his limbs had been ignited by a consciousness separate to his own. His hand grabbed the knife and his legs moved in a perfect pirouette. As he spun towards Rafa, his arm swung out fast and low, embedded the knife deep in Rafa's midriff, then pulled the blade sideways. Skin stretched and split, and opened like a monstrous mouth. The wound vomited blood. Intestines slipped out like eels spilling from a bucket. Walter released his grip and the knife clattered to the floor.

The two young men, such quick companions and friends, stood staring at each other in terror and wonder.

'Help me,' whispered the young Spaniard. He looked at his hands, slippery with blood and viscera as he tried to close the wound in his belly. Walter touched his friend's hand, then put an arm around his waist. 'Can you walk? I know where we can get help.' Gently, he led the injured man to the door. 'Careful you don't slip. Hold on to me now. We're almost there.' Walter opened the door and led Rafa out to the little walkway that led to the ship's stern.

'I am cold and frightened.'

Tears momentarily blinded Walter, but he shook his head and blinked fast a half-dozen times. 'Almost there.'

They stood at the stern. All around sea and sky merged like a vast black robe dusted with crushed diamonds. 'Step up here. That's right. Lean against the rail. Help is at hand. Close your eyes.' Walter bent down, put his arms around his friend's thighs and, with a violent grunt, lifted Rafa up and tossed him over the stern.

Shaking with horror, Walter turned around and saw a crouching figure silhouetted before the open door of his quarters. The figure stood up. As it stepped closer Walter realised it was the ship's captain. He looked at Walter, with his head cocked to one side. Walter held his arms out, the scarlet gore dripping from his fingers. 'Have you never seen blood?' the youth hissed. 'Help me clean up this mess and you will have my loyalty forever.'

'I'd rather your gold,' replied the captain.

'So be it.'

'Good, then let's be quick in our business.'

A week later, on a dark and rain-drenched morning, the two ships docked in Galway city. Word of Rafa's death had preceded the crafts' arrival. The facts, copied from the ship's log, stated that one evening the captain had called on Walter and Rafa. Walter had accepted an invitation to inspect the ship. Rafa had remained behind. The Spaniard's mood was melancholy and he stated he was missing his home and family. When the captain and Walter returned two hours later Rafa was missing and the room in a state of disarray. Blood and wine stained the floor and walls; a glass and broken bottles lay scattered around; the small dining table was overturned, a plate, meat and bloody knife on the floor beside it. Following an inquiry the captain concluded Rafa had stolen the wine, drunk too much of it and, overcome by alcohol or remorse, had suffered injury before falling overboard. No other party was believed to be involved in the tragic death.

'It was unwise to keep such strong wine in your quarters,' was Mayor Lynch's response. He and Walter were sat again in the top storey room in Market Street office. 'But the man is dead and only God knows when the sea will release him for judgement. But that is the Lord's business, not ours. Our business is in guarding the life, structure and commerce of Galway. You going about black clad and pale skinned does nothing to build confidence.'

'Will you deny my right to mourn, father?'

'I mourned your mother, with good reason. Our marriage strengthened the bond between the Lynch and Blake families, which in turn enhanced the peace of the land. She provided me with a son and her advice on politics showed she was not without reasoning facilities. She was fair to look at. When she died I mourned as was proper, then returned to greater matters. You knew Rafa for only a few weeks. I do deny you the right to mourn him.'

Walter looked from his father to the mahogany table and, to his horror, saw it was covered in splinters of glass spattered with blood. He swallowed hard, took a breath, and willed the blood and glass to become nothing more than rubies and pearls. 'May I open the window, father?'

'You may.'

Clenching his fists, the young man walked across the room, opened the long window and secured it to the metal bracket. A cold wind blew in. It carried the smell of seaweed and fish.

'I will put aside my mourning, father.'

'That is well. I have written a letter to your late companion's uncle, expressing our sympathies and informing him a service will be held in St Nicholas'. For now, we must discuss business. I am pleased with how you conducted yourself in Malaga. The wine is exceptionally fine and the price good. My accountant has vouched your book keeping. By way of reward I have decided to let you keep half of the money remaining. In addition, I have already sold the wine on your behalf and, as agreed, all that profit will go to you. I suggest a bonus to your crew and a donation to St Nicholas'.'

The years following Walter's return from Spain saw the fortune of the youth increase in tandem with his reputation. Though he returned to wearing the attire of a young dandy, he indulged in no other youthful frippery or waywardness. He attended church daily. Such was his devotion that often he would be overcome with a terrible shaking fit, his response to which was to press his hands tightly together as he prayed fervently to Mary, Mother of God and Queen of Heaven. Yet devotion to the Church and Heaven did not impinge on his devotion to trade and politics. In his own way he was as astute as his father, and between them the stern patrician and the devout son kept a firm grasp on the fortune and future of Galway and its inhabitants.

Father and son lived in remarkable times. The world was shrinking as merchants sought to follow Columbus. From England ships such as the *Bristol* and *George* came seeking Hy Brazil to establish a foothold in the vast Atlantic, whilst Ferdinand and Isabella, the monarchs of Catholic Spain, fretted that England would capture the elusive island first. Outside the walls of Galway city the great Gaelic and English families made and broke alliances, and spilled blood in battle and assassination, whilst the English King vowed to bring Ireland fully under his control. In the midst of this, the mayor and his son proved adroit at playing off the innumerable adventurers, assassins, factions, monarchists and merchants operating in Galway.

Where once the mayor's rivals sought means to destroy the Lynch family, now they competed with one another in a different game: marrying a daughter off to Walter Lynch. However, as every sailor knows, Lady Luck is a capricious creature. One moment her hand on the rudder conscientiously steers a ship or a family through safe and calm seas, and then with a twitch she steers all into rocky shallows.

The captain who bartered his silence for gold fell ill. His sickness was sudden, weight fell from his frame, and overnight his sturdy limbs became as thin and fragile as kindling. With death approaching he called for his priest and his family. 'I cannot die with such a stain on my soul. I bore witness to murder yet held my tongue. I saw Walter Lynch kill his Spanish companion.'

The captain's words seeped out from his home and into the streets and lanes of Galway. By the following morning not a soul in the city and county of Galway was ignorant of the dying man's accusation. At mid-morning, Mayor Lynch called for his son, for the town's bailiffs and for the warden of St Nicholas' church. They met at noon in the room looking over Market Street. The window was open. The thoroughfare below filled rapidly as people gathered in anxious assembly. The murmur of their conversations rose like a tide that spilled into the room in a verbal flotsam of Irish, English, Spanish, French and Dutch. While few words or phrases could be clearly discerned, the rising sound carried a sense of fear and panic.

The mayor walked over to the window. Taking a moment to appreciate the vastness of the mob below him, he stepped on to the ledge. His presence commanded a silence: no one spoke and not a bird dared flutter its wings, or a dog whine. The city, the people, the animals, the very bricks and mortar, all waited for the mayor to speak.

'I stand here to condemn those who would spread such fearful rumour in our land. Fearful is the proper word. By seeking to destroy my son they seek to destroy all his work and deeds, and mine, and the work and deeds of every man, woman and child in Galway. They would destroy our prosperity and replace it with fearfulness and tyranny. They are fools, though, who think they can so attack us. My forefathers sacrificed much to build this city, to make it one of the greatest and richest sea ports in the world. I will do anything to protect that legacy. Not five minutes ago I placed my hand on a Bible and swore to hunt down and hang the enemies of my son, my family and Galway, whoever they may be, so help me God. As I speak my son stands in the company of our religious and secular authorities. He too will place his hand on that same sacred tome and swear his innocence. Then together, father and son, we will cleanse the city of this evil, no matter what it takes.'

As the crowd cheered, Mayor Lynch stepped back in to the room. Walter sat beside the small mahogany table. Behind him stood the men representing the highest legal and religious authority in Galway and on the table before them all lay a Bible. At the room door, packed tight together, stood representatives of the great families whose ancestors had founded the city three centuries ago. Among them stood the Blake patriarch, father of Mayor Lynch's deceased wife and grandfather of the young Walter Lynch.

As the young man reached out for the Bible, his face twisted as if in agony and he wrenched his hand back to his chest. The city's patricians watched in horror as Walter began to twitch and spasm, his legs and arms moving wildly of their own volition. Then, just as suddenly as they had begun, the convulsions stopped. Walter looked around the room. Later, many of the witnesses described his expression as being peaceful and resigned. He placed his hand on the Bible: 'I swear by God above and by Jesus our saviour who died to cleanse us of our sins that I killed my companion and friend Rafa the Spaniard.'

The words were no sooner spoken than they were repeated in the doorway and transmitted down five flights of stairs, spilling into every passing floor and out into the street. The news was met with groans and gasps and, very occasionally, muffled snorts of glee. Wagging tongues also told of how the mayor had staggered as if a great weight had crashed on to his shoulders. The mayor had indeed bent beneath the burden but he did not fall. His features as pale as a skull, he walked towards his son and declared, 'Justice will be done.'

The church warden put a hand on Walter's shoulder. 'Will you do penance?'

'And pay rightful compensation?' added the constable.

'I will,' replied the young man quietly.

Mayor Lynch shook his head. 'We here are the upholders of the law. Penance and compensation are not fit responses to such a crime.'

'Yes, they are,' said the Blake patriarch. 'We all know men who've done far worse yet have expurgated the sin through devout deeds and proper payment. Moreover, a man cannot be sentenced without proper trial.'

'The bailiffs are here. The warden of St Nicholas' church is here. And I, the magistrate of the city, am here. What more is needed?'

The patriarch made no reply. Instead, he whispered to one of his servants who turned and began pushing his way down the stairs. Noise erupted from the street as the populace responded to the breaking news with whistles and cries for clemency.

Mayor Lynch stood with his back to the window. The room echoed with the shouts and chants from the street rabble, yet the mayor's softly spoken words were perfectly audible to all present. 'As magistrate I declare Walter Lynch guilty of the crime of murder. He is sentenced to be taken beyond the walls of this city to a place of execution. There he shall have a rope placed around his neck and he shall be hanged until he is dead.

May the Lord have mercy on his soul. Bind his hands, constable. Bailiffs, lead the way.'

Walter did not speak as the constable bade him rise, turned him to face the door, then bound his hands behind his back with a thick piece of twine. A bailiff stood on either side of the young man, his father the magistrate behind him. Screams erupted from the street below. Walter's grandfather stood grim-faced in the doorway. He and the other men packed there refused to step aside.

'Reconsider, man,' pleaded Blake. 'The city need not suffer such an awful spectacle. Walter was a foolish youth then. Now he is a respected and much-loved man. It would be a crime to kill him just to salve your wounded pride.'

'My pride has nothing to do with this. The youth you speak of was foolish, but the man he grew into had years aplenty in which to make confession and compensation. Instead he chose to harbour evil in his breast and, in doing so, sheltered an enemy of this city. Hanging is the only suitable punishment.'

'And how will you convey him to his place of execution? Even if I were to step aside, I cannot say the same for those pressing against me. Listen to the rage and sorrow outside. How would you get through them?'

As the two men spoke, the bailiffs on either side of Walter glanced at the young man. The prisoner trembled a little and tears welled in his eyes, yet his demeanour was calm.

'Then I'll hang him myself,' declared Lynch. 'Bailiff, open that oak chest and bring out a rope.'

Without a word one of the bailiffs obeyed the city magistrate. Walter's father tied one end of the rope to the metal bracket beside the open window. 'Come here Walter. Let us finish this business'. Like one mesmerised, the young man began to walk to his father. No one intervened. A yard from

his father the young man's legs buckled and he fell to the
floor like a broken mannequin. He sat there for a moment
with a dumb expression on his face. He could see his father
standing with the rope in his hand. He could hear voices
screaming his name, but he was as uncomprehending as an
ox in a slaughter yard.

Then he looked at the window and understanding began
to return. Before him he saw the silhouette of someone
crouched down. Slowly the shaded figure stood up, shaking
as if from a some great physical or emotional effort, and
revealed itself. There stood Rafa, his belly ripped wide, but
his face pale and beautiful. He held out a blood-soaked hand.

'Don't worry my friend. Death is very easy.' Walter stood.
The vision vanished.

The young man waited patiently whilst his father secured
the rope around his neck.

'Step up here, son.'

Walter stepped on to the ledge. The stone, the air and the
rope around his neck buzzed and vibrated with the sound of
horrified shrieks and howls from below.

'None dare defy me!' the mayor roared to the crowd below
as he pushed his son from the ledge.

Death is easy. Dying is not. Walter dangled from the
window, choking and twisting, for fifteen minutes. The crowd
that had been so animated and enraged became mute as they
stared, mesmerized, at the diabolical drama above them. In the
window frame stood Mayor Lynch, his face twisted with rage
and defiance. Below him his son swung on the end of rope like
a gruesome pendulum. His body bucked and twitched, his face
turned black and blood spilled from his bulging eyes.

Some of the mob tried to grab his feet, hoping, if not to save
him, at least to yank hard enough to snap the lad's neck and

end his suffering. But as hands reached for Walter's feet, Mayor Lynch tightened his grip on the rope.

'Is that your game,' he yelled. Hand over hand he pulled his son's still living and suffering body upwards, and then, with a laugh, lowered it down again.

As an angler in the Corrib will tease a salmon with the bait, flashing it before the fish then snatching it away, so Lynch teased the men, women and children of his city. For a quarter of an hour he played his game; letting his choking and gargling son drop to the crowd, then snatching him upwards again. When the body stopped twitching, he untied the rope and let the corpse fall. Panting and sweat-smeared from exhaustion, the mayor turned to look at the spectators in his room. 'None dare defy me.'

The horror of that day ensured Mayor Lynch retained his position of eminence in the city. Who indeed would dare defy a man who could simultaneously kill his son and mock his detractors? Yet no man is Immortal and James Lynch, mayor, magistrate and merchant, had only a few years in which to enjoy his new notoriety. Whether they be princes or paupers, all men die and are lowered lifeless into the ground. So it was with Mayor Lynch, and it was said by some that the rope used to lower his coffin in to the ground was the very same rope that he himself had used to hang his own son.

17

THE CITY
BENEATH THE WAVES

There are two weeks of the year when Galway Bay fills with mackerel, swimming in their millions upon millions, chasing the quick silver galaxies of tiny darting sprats. And just as they eat the sprats, there are fellows who eat the mackerel. Seals can be seen at that time of the year, out in the bay, swallowing fish after fish until their bellies are near bursting. Then, of course, there are the fishermen of the Claddagh, to whom the mackerel are a blessing, some say, from McDara the saint who watches over fisherfolk.

Well, one July morning, a hundred years ago or so the cry went out: 'The mackerel are running.' There was great excitement amongst all the fishing crews, but none were as excited as the three young O'Hara brothers. Every trip out they had sailed with their father, but on this day the old fellow was ill in the stomach and the head. Confined to bed, he told his sons he was sure they had the skills and the brains now to take out his boat themselves.

This filled the lads with pride, and they were all eager to go out and make their first catch without their father. They stowed the nets in the boat and checked its sails, made sure there was food for the journey and fresh water to drink. All along the bay, men and boys were doing the same and the air was filled with the sounds of their shouts, whistles and laughter. But then, just as the boats were about to sail, a curious thing happened.

The O'Hara boys were busy at their tasks when they heard a commotion from further up the Claddagh. The lads looked up and saw an old woman astride a white horse coming along the shore, waving one arm in consternation and calling for all the men of the Claddagh to listen to her.

The lads watched as the woman trotted her horse down to the shore, got off the creature and approached the first of the boats. She put a hand on the arm of one fellow and said, 'Do not go out fishing this day'. But the fellow shook her off with a laugh, and told her to be on her way and take her nonsense with her. Along she went to the next boat, and the next. And at each of them she made her plea, and at each the men chided her and chased her off. The men told each other the woman was cracked, maybe from age or hunger, or just plain disposition. But the woman was neither a fool nor an innocent. She was as clever as any woman ever born, and every bit as determined that her opinion should be heeded.

Along all the boats, all four score and more, she went, demanding the fishermen listen to her. But the sun had broken free of the horizon and the mackerel were jumping with even greater fervour, and as she went each and every crew would push her away, leap into their boats, set a fine red sail around a passing breeze and sail off into the bay. Eventually there was only one boat left, and that was the one being fitted out by the three young O'Hara boys.

By now the woman's voice was thin and sore from pleading, but she tried, nonetheless, to catch the attention of the boys. 'Men of the Claddagh,' she started, her voice not much above a whisper. Now, it so happened that no one had ever called the lads 'men' before. Their chests puffed out to be addressed as such, and so it was that they took a moment to ask the old woman what it was that was bothering her. The old woman pointed out to Galway Bay and this is what she said: 'There's a storm being born out in the Atlantic. It will come ashore at the Cliffs of Moher and then climb over the Burren, getting angrier and angrier from the effort of its climbing. When it drops down on Galway Bay the temper on it will be blacker and fiercer than the Devil himself.'

There was never a more perfect day for casting a net, the lads told the old woman, 'Look at the sun boiling away there like a big egg when yir hungry,' said the youngest brother.

'And the sky so blue and blinking at us,' said the middle one.

'And the breeze just perfect for fishing but without a hint of malice in it,' the older of the O'Hara lads added.

The old woman shook her head at the folly of men and said, 'If you must go fishing, would you do one thing for me?' The lads were impatient now to get the sails up and the boat out, so they agreed to do the woman one favour. 'My soul will rest easier tonight,' the old woman said, ' if you take on your voyage an axe, a hook, and a long sharp knife.' The lads agreed to this and sent the youngest brother back to the house to fetch the three implements. When all three O'Hara lads were aboard, with the axe, the hook and the long sharp knife for company, they set their boat out into the bay.

Well, the fishing was good, with the mackerel playing their part in the affair like good and honourable fish should, each creature leaping into whatever net was passing through their locality. By early afternoon there was not a boat that was not heavy with its load of mackerel packed tight and twitching, and glittering in the summer sunlight. And all the men and boys of the Claddagh were content and ready for home, and if any of them recalled the warning of the old woman, doubtless they made a joke of it, or perhaps, being in good fettle, wished her innocent self well.

But just as the boats turned for home the heat left the day and a shiver touched every soul and sail upon the water. A black line appeared in the sky just above the Burren, as if the air was frowning. Then the breeze stopped, the sails sagged, and the men and boys looked fearfully as that dark frown spread like ink or black blood. Before any man could shout out a warning, the storm was on them, roaring like an army, throwing men and boats every which way and the other. Lightning stabbed at the boats like the silver fork of a god hungry for his victuals. And the winds were there from every corner of the world – North, South, East and the West – tumbling and fighting each other in their eagerness to wreck the most boats. The air was so thick with the spray of the waves and the battering of the rain that there were men who drowned even as they stood firm on deck, grasping fast on to the masts of their boats.

The O'Hara brothers struggled to steer for home, but one black-bellied wave rose up above the rest. Twice the size of a house it was, and roaring and spitting like a creature alive as it threw itself at the O'Hara lads. Well, without even thinking, the oldest boy grabbed the axe, shouted out 'God keep us from harm!', and threw it at the giant wave. The very second the blade of the axe touched the wave it parted in two like the Red Sea before Moses, and passed harmlessly by on either side of the boat.

But the deeps sent up an even greater swell of water, the size of a hill. Its belly was scarlet with anger and its brow was pricked with broken masts and limbs. Spiting and roaring, it reared up above the little boat. Without a moment's thought, the second boy grabbed the hook and shouted, 'God keep us from harm!' and threw it at the giant wave. The moment the

hook touched the wave, it parted in two like the Red Sea before
Moses, and the lads were once more saved.

The third wave though was as high as Mweelrea Mountain
up there in Killary and its belly was filled with silver lighten-
ing. Yet, except for a low rumbling, the monster was almost
silent. On it came, determined to carry out its hellish duty,
when up stood the youngest boy, all thirteen years of age,
and did he not grasp the long sharp knife, cry out 'God keep
us from harm!' and throw the knife at the terrible beast of a
wave. Sure enough, the moment the knife touched the wave
it parted in two like the Red Sea. As one half of it passed
meekly by the portside, and the other just as meek by the
starboard, it left behind a gentle swell that pushed the O'Hara
boat all the way home.

As they sailed into the Claddagh, the wind died down and
the rain turned softer. Yet even now, their adventure was only
half done. For standing on the shore was the old woman and
her horse, with not a drop of dampness on them. 'You cannot
step ashore,' spoke the old woman as the lads tied their boat
fast, 'unless you sit on my horse and follow me.' Up the three
of them mounted, none of them daring to ask questions of the
woman, even when she started walking into the waves with the
horse at the side of her.

Under the water they went, following the stones and sand
and rocks, down and down below Galway Bay, until they came
to a handsome city set with buildings made from the finest
Connemara marble. As the horse trotted through the under-
water city, the lads could hear distant singing and laughter,
and fiddles and pipes playing merry jigs. The gay sound grew
clearer and louder, and then the woman led the lads into a
great park filled with dancing merrymakers. But the boys had
no time to take a proper look at the people dancing there, for

the old woman was now hurrying the horse along to a great mansion in the middle of the park.

When they reached the front of the house, the old woman bade the lads jump down from the horse and said, 'Now you must go in here. And when you are inside you must do exactly as I tell you, and you must not utter even a single word! Inside the house there is a flight of stairs which lead up to a landing that has three doors on it. Each of you must go into one of those rooms, and take from it what is yours. But, only what is yours.'

The three lads stepped into the house. The oldest of the boys went up the stairs and opened the first room. Inside was a bed and lying on the bed, the most beautiful woman he had ever seen, with hair as black as the belly of the first wave. The lad gasped in horror as he saw embedded in her forehead the axe he had thrown. The lad forced himself to stand over the woman, grasped the axe's wooden handle and tugged. With a terrible wet sound the axe came free and the lad staggered back clutching it, all the while staring in wonder as the wound on the woman's head healed over until there was not a mark on her.

The woman opened her eyes and sat up. 'Thank you,' she said. But the boy did not utter a word in reply. 'Thank you for healing my terrible wound,' she said, holding out her hand. Lying on her palm was a necklace made from large white pearls. 'For you,' she said, smiling. The pearls seemed to grow ever larger as the boy stared at them, thinking that if he ever took them to Galway city he would be sure to find a girl marry him. The boy closed his eyes, gripped ever tighter onto the axe-handle and stepped backwards towards the door. Then he reached one hand behind him, opened the door, stepped through it and slammed it shut. With that, the spell was broken and he ran down the stairs to his brothers.

Up then went the second boy, and into the next room. Inside was a bed with a beautiful woman laying on it, with hair as scarlet as the belly of the second wave, and sticking out from her head the gleaming curve of the hook. The boy gulped back his horror, reached down and pulled the hook out. With that the wound on the woman's forehead healed, her eyes opened and she sat up. 'Thank you,' she said. 'You must be hungry after your terrible day'. She clicked her fingers and a table appeared covered in platters of meat, bowls of fruit, and goblets of champagne. Well, the boy had never felt so hungry in his life and his mouth filled with saliva, but though his stomach grumbled he gripped the hook's handle all the harder, stepped backwards, opened the door and left. The second the door slammed shut, the spell was broken and he too ran down the stairs.

The final lad, the youngest, not more than thirteen years of age, now stepped into the last room. There was a bed and on it a beautiful woman, with hair as silver as the belly of the third wave, and embedded deep in her forehead was the long sharp knife. The boy grabbed the knife's handle and tugged. So deep was it in her head that he had to tug harder and harder, until, with a terrible noise of metal scraping against bone, it came out from her skull. As the wound healed up, the woman's eyes opened, and as she sat up she looked at him. 'Thank you,' she whispered, and patted the bed.

The boy held the handle of the knife as tight as he could, but felt his will soften at the woman's gentle whispers, urging him to sit beside her. Whilst he managed to stop any words spilling out from him, he had no power to stop himself walking over to the bed and sitting down on it. The woman bent closer to him and whispered in his ear, 'Have you ever kissed a girl?' She put her hand on his chin and turned him to face her. Now the boy's heart was pounding, blood roared around his body, and his belly filled with fire of passion as he bent into the embrace of the woman.

Just then the room of the door burst opened with a mighty crash. In ran the two older lads, who grabbed their youngest brother just as his lips were about to touch those of the temptress and dragged him across the room, threw him out on to the landing and slammed the door shut behind them. And with that the spell was broken.

All three came down the stairs bringing with them the axe, the hook and the long sharp knife. When they were outside the house, the old woman nodded at them and said, 'now you can go home'. The three lads sat back on the horse and the old woman led them away from the house. As they crossed the park the music was louder and they could see clearly the dancers around them. Everywhere they looked they saw smiling women, each as enchanting as the three they had escaped from. And dancing with the women were the fishermen of the Claddagh.

It was night when they arrived home, the storm long gone, and the sky was filled with twinkling stars. The three lads got off the horse and stood silently beside the old woman, looking at the bits of wood floating on the quiet waves, listening to the sounds of weeping coming from the Claddagh's darkened homes. 'Is it only us three who survived?' asked the eldest brother. The old woman nodded.

'But surely' pleaded the youngest, 'the dancing must finish sometime, and then the others can also come home.'

'The seas will have long dried up before that music stops,' replied the old woman.

'But why us,' asked the middle boy, 'why have we survived?'

The old woman just shrugged her shoulders. All three boys, their voices cracking with emotion, tears spilling from their eyes, insisted that there had to be a reason why they survived. Any reason at all.

The old woman looked at each of them and then said, 'If you need a reason for why you survived, perhaps it is this: you three, and you three only, took the time to listen to an old woman from the Claddagh.'

And with that she got up on her horse and rode back into the sea, never to be seen again.

TOBY'S
WISH

Many people visiting Ireland or coming to the island to embark on a new life endeavour to involve themselves in the local culture. And there is much to join in with: language, dance, exploring the ancient tombs, climbing Croagh Patrick. But of course, the one aspect of Irish culture that stands out more than any other is its music.

Ireland is a country with a tremendous fecundity of songs and music. There are songs to cover all situations: love, battles, mammy, exile, drinking and death – many of the best tunes being a combination of two or three of these. And, of course, to accompany the singing of these songs there is an abundance of musical instruments: fiddles, uilleann pipes, squeeze boxes, guitars and whistles. But, curiously, the most important instrument of them all is the one that is given the least respect – and that is the bodhrán.

The bodhrán is best compared to those plain pieces of thread that hold a golden wedding gown together. Everybody and their aunt may comment on the finery of the dress but if the plain old bits of thread were not there then all that silk and satin would be nothing more than a pile of radiant rags gathered round the dainty feet of a blushing bride. And so it is with the bodhrán. It is the bodhrán that allows every individual note of a melody to find its proper place in the tune; the correct fold and weave, and rise and dip, as it where. Without the bodhrán the melody would collapse. Yet the bodhrán is so taken for granted that few make note of its crucial and fundamental role in the life and culture of Ireland.

Now there was a lovely young man came to Ireland from America in the late 1970s. His name was Toby; he was a tall young lad of only nineteen years or so. He had tousled hair, sparkling eyes and a wonderful smile that was filled with fine teeth, the likes of which were whispered about in rumours but seldom seen in reality. His ancestors had come from Ireland, so it was only fitting that he should return here to try and gain some understanding of his roots and heritage.

Toby was desperate to involve himself in some way with Irish culture and figured a good start would be to savour a bit of the *craic agus ceol*, which is to be found in the many and diverse watering holes of the island. To this end he bought himself a bodhrán, thinking that it would be easy enough to make a tune out of a stick and a bit of goat skin. And here was the folly and the tragedy of Toby of the fine teeth. Perhaps, if fate had been kinder, he may eventually have come to understand that the bodhrán is not only the heartbeat and the fabric of all Ireland's greatest tunes, but is also one of the most difficult and deceptive of instruments to play.

But Toby had bought a bodhrán and off he went. Wherever he found a session he would join in with his elbow leaping up and down and his fist pounding away as he brought all his youthful optimism and vigour to the playing of his bodhrán. If a tune was soft and subtle he skelped his way through it like a rampaging elephant. If the music was fast he whizzed along then spluttered to a stop midway, took a breath then whizzed on again without the slightest observation of any changes in the pace of the tune.

Some of the men around him would give him a dunt; others, being more diplomatic, would ply him with drink in the hope that the alcohol would either knock him unconscious or kick start the vital spark that would allow the poor lad to finally play his chosen instrument well.

To begin with, nobody threatened him; he was such a likeable lad, funny, polite and full of a boundless sense of wonder. And, of course, his teeth were a wonder to behold. People would come into a bar just to see the flash and perfection of his pearly whites. The women of Ireland were particularly taken with Toby, his charm and his flashing smile. Indeed many of *mbann na heireann* fell hopelessly in love with the youth, and he, being a gentleman, took it upon himself to love as many of them back as was humanly possible.

Soon enough, what with the lousy bodhrán playing and his vigorous appreciation of the ladies, the men of Ireland grew weary of the lad. So it was that he found himself chased out of every village, hamlet, town and city in Ireland, until at last he came to the one place on the island where you can play your bodhrán as badly as you want and kiss as many ladies as you want without anybody batting an eyelash, and that of course is the great Sodom and Gomorrah of Connemara, commonly known as Galway City.

He had only been in the city for a day when he stumbled on a session in the Crane bar on Williams Street. Not so long ago farmers and merchants would tie up their carts along the length of the street to do a day's exchanging of goods, money and gossip. Then, with business concluded and local lads feeding and watering the ponies, the men would retire into the adjoining hostelries for a satisfactory swig and sing-along. By the time Toby swaggered into the Crane bar, the era of the ponies and carts had long faded, but the music was as fresh and as joyous as ever.

In went Toby of the flashing teeth and out came his bodhrán. A session was in full swing, with the music and the black stuff spilling merrily all over the place. Fiddles sang, whistles peeped, singers laughed and lamented. Toby's complete disregard for tune and tone was, for once, met with tolerance, encouragement and good cheer. In a room full of men and women with teeth like cracked and mouldy tombstones, Toby's flashing teeth were a passport to tolerance and conviviality.

One young woman was particularly taken with Toby. Her name was Peggy and she was as pretty as a star in the twilight, and as sweet as a flower in the morning. Many a glance she cast Toby's way, with all the precision and skill of an angler courting a salmon. Dawn was not far off when the celebrants staggered and sang their way from the pub. Peggy, seeing her chance, put a hand on Toby's arm and asked, 'would you like to come for a walk with me? There is nothing as beautiful as the banks of the Corrib early in the morning.'

Off the pair walked, in a meandering perambulation, by the Eglinton canal and on to the university. Then past that great place of learning and onto the path that leads to Dangan. To the right of them, the Corrib could be glimpsed through clusters of trees. Soon the young pair they were walking arm-in-arm, full of happiness and hormones, and chatting away delightfully about everything and nothing.

'Have you ever seen fairies?' Toby asked his beautiful companion.

'Oh sure, you can't move for the feckers.'

'Could I get to see one?'

'Eh …'

'I would do anything to see a real live Irish fairy.'

'Ah well, I do know a place where they hang out. They're a bit shy, so you might not actually see one, but if you make a wish it may come true.'

'That's awesome. How do we get there?'

'Oh, it's not too far. Close your eyes and take my hand.'

Toby did so and the ever-resourceful Peggy led him to a little narrow dirt track on the right that meandered towards a line of trees. On an overhead branch sat a fine-looking starling. It chest was speckled and its eyes clever. It cocked its head to see what was causing all the rustling and snapping below him.

'Careful now, the path goes down here.'

Toby tightened his grip and Peggy's heart leapt. Peggy led Toby through a patch of thick undergrowth and then down a steep incline.

'Here we are!'

Toby opened his eyes. He was standing in a small grassy hollow, round and shallow and carpeted with deep soft grass. On one side of the oval dip was the screen of trees Peggy had led him through. On the other side of was a line of boulders and, beyond them, the wide expanse of the Corrib River. Though the sky was now turning light, the water still held the evening's blackness. Toby gazed at the dark river and a chill went through him. The water seemed to be rising and falling ever so subtly, and had a thickness to it that made it look like a giant monstrous tongue.

'What do you think?' asked Peggy. Toby looked at her and his fear vanished. She had a smile on her face and a glint in her eye. As he looked on the pale and perfect face of Peggy, the world around slowed and faded into an insubstantial mirage.

'What do you wish for, Peggy?' whispered the young American.

The woman made no reply. Looking into Toby's eyes she unbuttoned her coat, took off her dress and lay down on the dew-glittered grass. Toby, ever the gentleman, disrobed and lay down beside her. The starling fluttered above them, but the young lovers were lost in the limbs and the breath of one another.

Later, Toby sat up and looked at the beautiful morning. The sky was blue, and the river was silver. The ever-resourceful Peggy gazed at her handsome lover and enjoyed a momentary vision of sky scrapers, a diamond ring and the green card of American citizenship. 'What do you wish for, Toby?'

Toby smiled a beautiful, perfect-toothed smile. Unabashed, he stood up and stretched. 'What do I wish for?' he whispered as he walked towards the boulders before the water's edge. He stood on one of the boulders and, turning to look at Peggy, declaimed: 'I wish for the entire world to cheer me on and roar its approval at my brilliance and genius!' Saying which, he punched his fist into the air, lost his balance and fell arse over tit into the Corrib River.

Grabbing her coat, Peggy leapt up and ran to the water's edge. Her lover was already far beyond her reach. 'Man in the water!' she screamed. Early morning anglers in small boats turned to were she was pointing. Toby's arm rose out of the water then vanished again, then up came his head and down it went. Further and faster down river went Toby, his position confirmed by the briefest flash of his leg, a glint of his belly. Then his arse stayed above water for a good few minutes, bopping up and down and smiling to the crowds gathering on the bank of the river.

As quick as a storm the word thundered down the river; 'Man in the water!' On Jordan Island an angler, seeing a chance for fame and glory, cast a line and briefly sank a barb into Toby's shoulder, but the water was not about to give up its little morsel. The line snapped and on Toby rolled.

Unconcerned, the water continued its journey, tumbling over the Salmon Weir and onwards, faster and more fulsome. Then under the narrow bridge that prisoners once filed pathetically across, but is now the thoroughfare of students, academics, shoppers and tourists. On that very bridge a crowd gathered to watch and debate the spectacle of Toby's watery journey. His body was still seen to be moving and a great and heated discussion ensued as to whether this showed the lad was still living, or was merely a result of the mischievousness nature of Galway's river.

A nun declared, 'When Cromwell was here didn't the holy sisters walk across the water just there and make it to safety?' Every man, woman, child, dog and member of the avian family looked to were she was pointing, but Toby did not rise up from the water.

On rolled Toby, under the O'Brien Bridge and down to the final bridge of Galway city. The Wolfe Tone Bridge was named after the revolutionary hero who in his younger days let his hair down in Galway Town and indulged in the timeless student pastimes of supping, singing and amateur dramatics. The horrified and the curious citizenry of Galway witnessed Toby passing beneath the solid stone arches. They ran to the opposite side of the bridge but no sign could be seen of Toby in the waters bursting and spitting out from the archways.

As the alert was transmitted by word, telephone and by off-shore radio, an extensive search began but no trace of Toby's body was found. 'He'll be on his way back to America,' explained a fisherman to the tearful Peggy later that day as she stood on the Wolfe Tone Bridge staring out at Galway Bay.

Toby's body had in fact passed beyond the ancient boundary of the city and into the magical domain of the Claddagh. Here, where the river widened into Galway Bay, every splash and spit of spray was alive with stories: princesses and hidden cities; battles between fisher folk and the British constabulary; mermaids and monsters; even the Devil himself was known to have paid the occasional visit. In a place so saturated with history and magic it was scarcely surprising that Toby's journey to Ireland now began to transform into something both horrific and wondrous. For though Toby was dead – his neck snapped and his lungs swollen with water – the river had determined that his adventure would continue for a little while longer.

Beyond Wolfe Tone Bridge Toby's folded-up corpse had become ensnared in a hole in the river bed. With the trunk of his body plugging up the hole, his sightless head lolled from side to side and his lifeless arms and legs waved about in the current like the tendrils of some monstrous anemone. As the days passed the bacteria in his gut grew hungry and, frustrated at the lack of nourishment, took to nibbling at Toby's stomach. Soon enough they'd chewed through the lining and spilled out into the great and boundless cave system of Toby's body. To the delight of the countless microscopic beings, boundless supplies of eatables were to be found in every niche and hollow of that fine cadaver.

Lacking any concept of restraint, finesses or table manners, the bacteria gorged themselves. A trillion new bacteria were born every day and they too quickly indulged in the delights of feeding, farting and fornicating.

Over the days and weeks the river water rose and fell and rose and fell in accordance with rains and tides, and the operation of the great metal sluices of the weir further upstream. The moon rolled round the earth, and the earth rolled round the sun, and all the while Toby's decaying body began filling up with gas.

The gas, in its turn, leaked out from the corpse's rearward orifice only to be trapped in the hole that was sealed shut by Toby's body. Slowly but surely, the pressure of the gas began to build. On those days when the river was low and the sun warm the gas became particularly agitated and little tremors would shudder through the cooling carcass. All the while, the carefree bacteria continued to indulge.

Bacteria were not the only carbon-based beings enjoying life to the full. Back on dry land many of the local bi-peds were buzzing with excitement too. In the cafes, bars, bedsits, attics and flophouses of Galway City, creative individuals were gathering together to discuss theatre, poetry, music, politics, Ireland, language, dance, the planet, painting and puppetry – and doubtless taking time to indulge in pastimes similar to their distant microscopic cousins. Across the city a great mass of energies – intellectual, physical, sexual, psychic, spiritual and profane – spun ever faster and faster. A body could not walk down Shop Street without tripping over a newly declaimed poem or a tuneful anarcho-syndicalist orchestration of household crockery.

Yet even as excitement grew, many recalled the terrible events of 1971 when unrestrained sparks of artistic philosophising became so hot and febrile that, so it was said, they ignited the timber in McDonogh's yard, setting off a conflagration that swallowed much of the city between Merchants Road and Williamsgate Street. Art was dangerous, and as the winter gave way to spring, a proposition was made by the University College Galway Arts Society that all the feverish machinations of the artistic community should be channelled safely into creating one great event that would blaze as bright as a supernova, but without the attendant shockwave of burning dust and gas.

So it was that on 6 April 1978 the very first Galway Arts Festival was launched under the title 'Galway Arts Society's Week of Crack'. It was a warm late spring day as a great and cosmopolitan mass of humanity came together at the Spanish Arch, a public area on the east bank of the city river directly opposite the Claddagh. The river was low. The air was warm. Stuck in its hole, Toby's body quivered. Back on land all manner of peoples were squeezed together: students, artists, tourists, gaelgoirs, Galwegians, drunks, pioneers, intellectuals, revolutionaries, feminists, under-cover police and the great and the good from as far afield as Enniscorthy in the south-east and Iqualuit in the north-west. As numbers swelled, the crowd spilled onto the nearby Wolfe Tone Bridge.

At the appointed moment a poet stepped on a box, opened his arms and announced in Irish and English the commencement of festivities. No sooner had the words left the rhymer's mouth than the waters of the river erupted with a great blast and Toby's body leapt into the air. Higher and higher the corpse flew as the crowds stared in amazement. Cameras clicked, fingers pointed, children were lifted up to get a better view. Three hundred feet in the air, the cadaver exploded, sending bones, skin and globules of fat hurtling out over Galway city, river and bay. Far below the crowds packed on Wolf Tone Bridge and the Spanish Arch roared and whooped in joy and exhilaration.

So it was that Toby's wish came true, and from that day till this there has never been an act as loudly acclaimed as the flying corpse of Toby the lousy bodhrán player.

Conclusion

I was aware as I wrote this book of how small it was when measured against the scope and vastness of stories, myths, histories, plays, poems, songs, rumours, lies, tall tales, anecdotes and other creative inventions connected to Galway Bay and the west of Ireland. There was much more that I could relate but if I had tried to tell all the stories, I would have never finished the book.

The Aran Islands, for example, are packed with tales. I did consider writing about St Brendan the Navigator as he prepared to leave the Aran Islands for a journey that would take him from the realms of known lands like Hy Brazil, to distant and unbelievable shorelines far to the north and west that we now call North America. But for the purpose of the 'Ancient Tales' the triumph of Christianity in the west of Ireland was the proper climax of an account stretching back 15 billion years. So Brendan and the later saints were omitted. Likewise, I omitted a fuller account of Brecan converting the pagans of County Clare, keeping only the tale that showed the very different approaches taken by him and Enda.

More troubling was the omission of Bridget from Christ's victory in the pagan west. In some accounts of Patrick's triumph over Cruachán Aigli he is aided by a bell given to him by Bridget. But which Bridget? There is Bridget the saint of healing and a Bridget the goddess of healing. I originally thought about introducing Bridget the goddess: as a healer it would be appropriate that she would do anything to end the conflict, including giving up divinity. Then I considered using St Bridget, only in my version I would emphasis her pagan background and make her a druid who converted to Christianity. This version would not be entirely out of keeping with her life as it is recorded. She did come from a pagan background, and worked for a druid. But in the end, with a humble apology to the deity and the saint, I decided not to include them in Patrick's story. To do so would have necessitated expanding the story to a far greater size. If you would like to know more about Bridget go and have a chat with Jennie at Bridget's Garden in Roscahill. Tell her Rab sent you along.

With regards to the Immortals, at least one of them could have been given a greater account in this book. Finnbheara quickly recovered his wits after the establishment of Christianity, one of his most famous seductions taking place in the early modern period when he stole away Eithne, the new wife of Lord Hacket, in Tuam and took her to his abode beneath Knockma. The tale as it has come down to us says much about Lord Hacket's attempts to rescue his wife. However, the central character, Eithne, is little more than a cypher.

I quickly realised that telling the story from her perspective would be a fascinating endeavour. What would Eithne have made of the crumbling bones that were all that remained of Moses' granddaughter? In what state of preservation would she find the body of that great fighter and fornicator Queen Mebd? How would she get on with Finnbheara's long-suffering wife Una? And what were her thoughts on the man himself? Was she kidnapped against her will by the King of the Connaught

Immortals, or did she, perhaps, share a little complicity? The more I considered Eithne, the more I realised the story would not fit into a short story format. Reluctantly, I put her aside for a later date.

There are, of course, other versions of the Eithne and Finnbheara affair, including a wonderfully Gothic oral version told by the storyteller Clare Muireann Murphy, in which Una is portrayed as a formidable and wily character. As I wrote previously, there is always another version of every story just around the corner.

જી

People, it goes without saying, are just as important resources as any amount of printed words, particularly when dealing with stories like the ones in this book. I was having trouble fixing a narrative around Patrick's time on Inchagoill, *Inis An Ghaill* – the Island of the Strangers. I knew Lugnad had died there, but I could not picture a story that would give proper weight and respect to his death. I took a break from writing and went for a coffee with Deirdre, who is the administrator in the Arts Office of the National University of Ireland, Galway.

When I asked Deirdre what she knew about Patrick and Inchagoill, she smiled and took out her phone. She and her daughter Lanah had visited the island in the summer. She showed me the photos of the trip. I looked at the vivid green of the island trees and the grey solid stone of the island monuments, and the story suddenly fell into place. Deirdre also informed me that an alternative meaning for Moycullen is 'the plain of holly'. Though the different traditions are not mutually exclusive – indeed the one may serve as poetic metaphor of the other – for the purposes of this book I have chosen the definition that emphasises the Tuatha de Danann prince, Uillinn.

A place I often visit, and occasionally tell stories in, is Galway Museum. As well as being a very welcoming place, its exhibits and talks provide an ongoing narrative of the social history of the city and the bay. When I was having trouble working out Westropp's approach to Irish terms it was Breandán O'Heaghra, the museum's deputy director, who gave me some advice on Irish grammar. Brendan McGowan, the museum's development officer, also gave me some pointers on Irish. Irish is a crucial and respected aspect of life and culture in the west. Fortunately, we now live in times were the eccentricities of Yeats or the occasional mistakes of Westropp would not be easily ignored. However, I admit that my Irish is poor and, whilst I have taken care to avoid any mistakes, some may have slipped through, for which I take entire responsibility and would welcome corrections.

Brendan McGowan also provided useful information on the culture of the Claddagh, which was of great help in two of the chapters: the Introduction to Part Two and Toby's Wish.

Another authority on the Claddagh is Dr John Cunningham, an historian based at the National University of Ireland (NUI), Galway. Galway is a vibrant and inspiring place to live, but part of its vitality is due to the efforts of men and women who have ensured that the darker and harder struggles in the city's history have not been forgotten. Whilst this narrative does not deal explicitly with these struggles, I have endeavoured in my stories to reflect an appreciation of this other aspect of the city and the bay. Chatting to John over coffee certainly helped in this, as did reading his *'A town tormented by the sea': Galway 1790–1914*.

The illustrations that complement the narrative are the work of my friend, the artist Marina Wild. Marina and I previously collaborated on a collection of adventure poems for children called *Pirates, Dragons and Moon Monsters*. Marina also provided the front cover for my on-going blog novel 'Marcus Marcus & the Hurting Heart'. It is always a delight to sit down and look at her latest quirky creation. I find that when I work with Marina, there is always a little part of my head wondering how she'll transform my written words into a visual representation. This, of course, has an impact on my own creative process, which I am very happy to acknowledge. As for her beautiful pictures, they can be admired and enjoyed as stories in their own right.

Other people deserve a mention in regards to the making of this book: Beth Amphlett, the editor at The History Press Ireland, for her patience; Cindy Dring at NUIG Health Promotion Service for allowing me the time to write the book; and as always Fionnuala Gallagher, the arts officer of NUI Galway, whose head is as full of cunning ideas as my own, and whose calm encouragement has aided my creativity for many years now.

But of course the most important people involved in the creation of this collection of stories are my wife and two children. The physical act of writing is a long and lonely process, with the attendant danger that the writer may simply vanish completely into the tale to the loss of his perspective and sanity. Whilst sanity is not crucial to creativity, a sense of perspective is. A writer needs to be able to step back, sometimes well back, from the work they are creating. Only then can they see what is working and what is not.

I am very lucky that my time-out involves playing, exploring, chatting and cooking with two very imaginative and energetic boys. They already know versions of most of these stories and much more besides. My sons, my two lovely Galway boys, are lucky to live in a country where, whilst so

much has gone wrong, there is limitless potential for great healing and empowerment. That Ireland should contain so many stories – and that those stories continue to live, change, adapt and spawn infinite new versions – is a reflection of the power and vast scope of dreams and imagination existing in this little fragment of our one small planet.

As our planet rolls and races around the sun, so clouds and stars roll and race over Galway Bay. Some mornings the moon follows the boys as they make their way to school and crèche, with Venus occasionally trailing along as well. In the evenings we sometimes stand at the boys' bedroom window and watch as the sky darkens and the first stars appear over Yeti Hill. The infinite stars were there before the children were born. The stars will be there when my Galway boys become Galway teenagers, Galway men and, who knows, maybe Galway fathers. The stories, and the infinite possibility of endless other stories, will also be there. Doubtless the lads will have their own versions, and may even add a tale or two of their own. Anything and everything is possible …

SOURCES

INTRODUCTION TO PART ONE

Corfield, Richard, *Lives of the Planets* (New York, 2007)

McKie, Robin, 'Enceladus: Home of Alien Lifeforms?'
The Observer (29 July 2012)

McLean, Malcolm & Dorgan, Theo (eds), *An Leabhar Mòr:
The Gaelic Tradition Behind The Book* (Gaillmh, 2005)

http://home.web.cern.ch

CHAPTER 1: AN FEAR MÓR

Douglas, M.S.V., Smol, J.P., Savelle, J.M. and Blais, J.M.,
'Prehistoric Inuit whalers affected Arctic freshwater eco-
systems', *Proceedings of the National Academy of Sciences*,
Vol. 101, No. 6 (2004)

Westropp, Thomas Johnson, 'A Study in the Legends of the
Connacht Coast, Ireland', *Folklore*, Vol. 28, No. 2 (1917)
(JSTOR). Online at www.jstor.org/stable/1255026

CHAPTER 2: GIANT LOVE

Westropp, Thomas Johnson, 'A Study in the Legends of the Connacht Coast, Ireland', *Folklore*, Vol. 28, No. 2 (1917) (JSTOR). Online at www.jstor.org/stable/1255026

CHAPTER 3: THE TIME LORDS

Dennehy, Emer, 'A Hot Property: The Morphology and Archaeology of the Irish Fulachta Fiadh', *JKAHS*, Series 2, Vol. 8 (2008)

Heaney, Marie, *Over Nine Waves: A Book of Irish Legends* (London, 1994)

Higgins, Jim 'Mesolithic Finds in Oughterard'. Online at www.oughterardheritage.org

Mullal, Erin, 'Letter from Ireland: Mystery of the Fulacht Fiadh', *Archaeology Magazine*, Vol. 65 (2012)

CHAPTER 4: HY BRAZIL

Heaney, Marie, *Over Nine Waves: A Book of Irish Legends* (London, 1994)

James, Simon, *The Atlantic Celts: Ancient People or Modern Invention?* (London, 2000)

CHAPTER 5: PERFECT WEAPONS

Heaney, Marie, *Over Nine Waves: A Book of Irish Legends* (London, 1994)

James, Simon, *The Atlantic Celts: Ancient People or Modern Invention?* (London, 2000)

Kyne, Mary, 'Orbsen – Ancient name of Lough Corrib'. Online at www.oughterardheritage.org

Chapter 6: Queen Medb and King Finnbheara

Geddes and Grossets, *Celtic Mythology* (based on text by Charles Squire) (Lanark, 2000)

Heaney, Marie, *Over Nine Waves: A Book of Irish Legends* (London, 1994)

Kinsella, Thomas, *The Táin* (Dublin, 1969)

Wentz, W.Y. Evans, *The Fairy-faith in Celtic Countries* (New York, 1911). Online at http://archive.org/details/fairyfaithincelt00evanrich

Mebh's palace rathcrogan www.megalithicireland.com/Rath%20Cruachan%20Rathcroghan.html

Rathcrogan www.rathcroghantours.com/

Knockma http://corofin.galway-ireland.ie/knockma.htm

Chapter 7: Medb Goes to War

Kinsella, Thomas, *The Táin* (Dublin, 1969)

Westropp, Thomas Johnson, R*ing-Forts in the Barony of Moyarta, Co. Clare, and Their Legends*. Online at www.clarelibrary.ie/eolas/coclare/history/ringforts/loophead_cuchullin_legend.htm

Chapter 8: Last of the Superheroes

Heaney, Marie, *Over Nine Waves: A Book of Irish Legends* (London, 1994)

Korff, Anne and O'Connell, Jeff, *Kinvara: A Rambler's Guide* (Galway, 1985)

www.loophead.ie

The Oghil Wedge Tomb (Leaba Dhiarmada agus Ghrainne): www.saintsandstones.net/stones-leabadhiarmada-journey. htm

'Public Art in Lawrencetown: Diarmaid and Gráinne', in Galway County Council website: http://www.galway.ie/en/ Services/ArtsOffice/PublicArt/PublicArtinLawrencetown/

Chapter 9: A Terrible Beauty

Ford, Patrick K., 'Aspects of the Patrician Legend', in Ford, Patrick K. (ed.) *Celtic Folklore and Christianity* (Santa Barbara, 1983)

Hood, A.B.E., *St. Patrick: His Writings and Muirchu's life* (London, 1978)

MacMullen, Ramsay, *Changes in the Roman Empire: Essays in the Ordinary* (Princeton, 1990)

Mitchell, Stephen, *A History of the Later Roman Empire, AD 284–641* (Oxford, 2007)

Ó Riordain CSsR, John J., *Early Irish Saints* (Dublin, 2001)

Ross, Anne, 'Ritual and the Druids', in Green, Miranda J. (ed.) *The Celtic World* (London, 1995)

Chapter 10: The Conquest of Cruachán Aigli

Ford, Patrick K., 'Aspects of the Patrician Legend' in
    Ford, Patrick K. (ed.) *Celtic Folklore and Christianity*
    (Santa Barbara, 1983)
Hughes, Harry, *Croagh Patrick: A Place of Pilgrimage, A Place of
    Beauty* (Dublin, 2010)
Inchagoill Island: www.congtourism.com/inchgll.htm
Westropp, Thomas Johnson, 'A Study in the Legends of the
    Connacht Coast, Ireland', *Folklore*, Vol. 28, No. 2 (1917)
    (JSTOR)

Chapter 11: Satan's Last Redoubt

Westropp, Thomas Johnson, 'A Study in the Legends of the
    Connacht Coast, Ireland', *Folklore*, Vol. 28, No. 2 (1917)
    (JSTOR). Online at www.jstor.org/stable/1255026

Chapter 12: Enda and Brecan

Ó Riordain CSsR, John J., *Early Irish Saints* (Dublin, 2001)
Robinson, Tim, *Oileáin Árann: A Companion to the Map of the
    Aran Islands* (Galway, 1996)
Westropp, Thomas Johnson, 'A Study in the Legends of the
    Connacht Coast, Ireland', *Folklore*, Vol. 28, No. 2 (1917)
    (JSTOR). On line at www.jstor.org/stable/1255026

Chapter 13: Infinite Possibilities

McGarry, Patsy, 'Church stance on abortion and soul of child has varied over time', *The Irish Times* (20 November 2012)

Mac Niocaill, Gearóid, *Ireland before the Vikings* (Dublin, 1972)

Introduction to Part Two

Cunningham, John, *'A Town Tormented by the Sea': Galway, 1790–1914* (Dublin, 2004)

Montefiore, Simon Sebag, *Jerusalem: The Biography* (London, 2011)

Rice, Eugene F., Jr, *The Foundations of Early Modern Europe, 1460–1559* (London, 1970)

Walsh, Paul, *Discover Galway* (Dublin, 2001)

Chapter 15: Connor Quinn and the Swan Maiden

Westropp, Thomas Johnson, *County Clare Folk-Tales and Myths*. Online at www.clarelibrary.ie

Chapter 16: The Mayor's Window

Cantarino, Geraldo, 'An Island Called Brazil', *History Ireland*, Vol. 16, Issue 4 (2008)

Walsh, Paul, *Discover Galway* (Dublin, 2001)

Westropp, Thomas Johnson, 'A Study in the Legends of the Connacht Coast, Ireland. Part II', *Folklore*, Vol. 28, No. 4 (31 December 1917), (JSTOR). Online at http://www.jstor.org/stable/1255489

'The Warden of Galway (The Execution of Walter Lynch)', *Dublin Penny Journal*, Vol. 1, No. 29 (12 January 1833). Online at http://www.jstor.org/stable/30003107

Chapter 17: The City beneath the Waves

Thomson, David, *The People of the Sea* (Edinburgh, 1998)

Westropp, Thomas Johnson, 'A Study in the Legends of the Connacht Coast, Ireland', *Folklore*, Vol. 28, No. 2 (1917) (JSTOR). Online at http://www.jstor.org/stable/1255026

Chapter 18: Toby's Wish

Kenny, Tom 'Some Galway Fires', *Galway Advertiser* (24 June 2010)

Westropp, Thomas Johnson, 'A Study in the Legends of the Connacht Coast, Ireland. Part II', *Folklore*, Vol. 28, No. 4 (31 December 1917) (JSTOR)

Galway Arts Festival archives, Hardiman Library, National University of Ireland, Galway: http://archives.library.nuigalway.ie/col_level.php?col=T5

ABOUT THE AUTHOR

Rab Fulton is a professional storyteller and author. He is a member of Storytellers Ireland and his 'Celtic Tales' storytelling sessions have a growing local and international reputation and have featured on RTÉ Nationwide, RTÉ Radio's The Tubridy Show and Arena. In 2007 he was awarded the Deis Award for his storytelling work. For more on Rab's work see http://rabfultonstories.weebly.com/.

If you enjoyed this book, you may also be interested in …

Dublin Folk Tales

BRENDAN NOLAN

Have you heard the story of 'Bang Bang' Dudley, who roamed the streets of Dublin shooting anyone who caught his eye? Or of 'Lugs' Brannigan, the city's most famous detective? Do you know who the real Molly Malone was, or the story of Marsh's Library, or how the devil himself came to the Hellfire Club? These and many more accounts of Dubliners and Dublin City fill this book.

978 1 84588 728 5

Waterford Folk Tales

ANNE FARRELL

Included in this collection of tales from across the county are the tales of the legendary figures of Aoife and Strongbow, St Declan and the three river goddesses, together with stories of some of the less well-known characters such as Petticoat Loose, whose ghost is said to still roam the county, and the Republican Pig, who was unfortunate enough to become caught up in the siege of Waterford.

978 1 84588 757 5

Donegal Folk Tales

JOE BRENNAN

Donegal has a rich heritage of myths and legends which is uniquely captured in this collection of traditional tales from the county. Discover the trails where Balor of the Evil Eye once roamed, the footprint left by St Colmcille when he leapt to avoid a demon and the places where ordinary people once encountered devils, ghosts, and fairies.

978 1 84588 767 4

Visit our websites and discover thousands of other History Press books.

www.thehistorypress.ie
www.thehistorypress.co.uk